P9-DXH-801

Caught in the Act

Caught in the Act

by **PETER MOORE**

Viking

VIKING
Published by Penguin Group
Penguin Young Readers Group, 345 Hudson Street, New York, New York 10014, U.S.A.
Penguin Group (Canada), 10 Alcorn Avenue, Toronto, Ontario, Canada M4V 3B2
(a division of Pearson Penguin Canada Inc.)
Penguin Books Ltd, 80 Strand, London WC2R 0RL, England
Penguin Ireland, 25 St Stephen's Green, Dublin 2, Ireland (a division of Penguin Books Ltd)
Penguin Group (Australia), 250 Camberwell Road, Camberwell, Victoria 3124, Australia
(a division of Pearson Australia Group Pty Ltd)
Penguin Books India Pvt Ltd, 11 Community Centre, Panchsheel Park, New Delhi – 110 017, India
Penguin Group (NZ), Cnr Airborne and Rosedale Roads, Albany, Auckland, New Zealand
(a division of Pearson New Zealand Ltd)
Penguin Books (South Africa) (Pty) Ltd, 24 Sturdee Avenue, Rosebank,
Johannesburg 2196, South Africa

Penguin Books Ltd, Registered Offices: 80 Strand, London WC2R 0RL, England

First published in 2005 by Viking, a division of Penguin Young Readers Group

10 9 8 7 6 5 4 3 2 1
Copyright © Peter Moore, 2005

LIBRARY OF CONGRESS CATALOGING-IN-PUBLICATION DATA
Moore, Peter, date–
Caught in the act / Peter Moore.
p. cm.
Summary: Everyone believes that sophomore honors student Ethan Lederer is a top-notch scholar and a
great guy, but a new student helps Ethan to discover and disclose that he is just acting a role, even as she
reveals her own mental instability.
ISBN 0-670-05990-0 (hardcover)
[1. Self-realization—Fiction. 2. Theater—Fiction. 3. Mental illness—Fiction. 4. Family life—Fiction.
5. High schools—Fiction. 6. Schools—Fiction.] I. Title.
PZ7.M787515Cau 2005
[Fic]—dc22
2004014906

Book design by Jim Hoover
Printed in U.S.A.
Set in Cochin

Again,

to Hedy and Jake,

with all my love

{Dramatis Personæ}

ETHAN LEDERER, *student, actor*
JANE LANDAU, *student, girlfriend to Ethan*
LYDIA KRANE, *student, actor*

AMANDA, *sister to Ethan*
MOM, *mother to Ethan*
DAD, *father to Ethan*

RYAN KRANE, *brother to Lydia*
MAUREEN KRANE, *mother to Lydia*

TIM, SCOTT, NORA, *friends to Ethan*

JORDAN PAUL WHITING, *student, thespian*
Diverse THESPIANS, *including Bridget, Simone, Steven*
MR. LOMBARDI, *teacher of drama, director, & playwright*
MR. DUGAN, *teacher of chemistry*
MS. WAGNER, *teacher of English*
MS. ROSEN, *teacher of history*
MRS. HARTIGAN, *principal*
MR. MATONE, *counselor*

RANDALL, *tattoo artist*
DETECTIVE ECKHART, *an officer of the law*

Students, actors, merchants, townspeople, doctors of medicine.

[SCENE: *town of West Baring*]

CLOUDY ME

It was a cool day in October when Lydia Krane walked into our sophomore honors chem class. I was doomed from the minute I set eyes on her.

She walked over to Mr. Dugan and handed him the admit slip. All eyes were on her. She wasn't your typical West Baring High student. She had on black cargo pants and a black long-sleeved shirt. The color scheme was completed by her black boots and her blunt-cut black hair, obviously dyed. I couldn't see much of her face, which was hidden behind raven wings of hair.

"This is Linda Krane. She's new," Mr. Dugan said. "Welcome, Linda."

"Actually, it's Lydia," she said. She had a British accent.

"Oh, really? It says Linda."

"It's a mistake," she said. "I go by Lydia."

"Good enough. Lydia. Let me get you a book."

She looked at the floor while Mr. Dugan went to the closet to get her a textbook. She rubbed the crimson polish on her thumbnail.

"Here you go. Why don't you have a seat right back there by Ethan," he said, pointing to the seat next to me.

"Thank you much," she said. As she walked away from him, it looked to me like he was looking at her with the same curiosity as I was.

She took an empty seat near me.

"All right, let's get back to these problems," Mr. Dugan said. He pointed to the equation on the board: $AgNO_3 + Cu \rightarrow Cu(NO_3)_2 + Ag$. "So silver goes from plus one to zero oxidation state, but to account for everything, the electrons need to be placed into the half reaction." He wrote on the board: $e- + Ag^+ \rightarrow Ag^0$. "This is reduction. You see how the other half reaction is that of copper." He wrote: $Cu^0 \rightarrow Cu^{+2} + 2$ e-. "This is oxidation. Now you take it from here. Finish this and the other problems."

Everyone turned back to their work. All you could hear were pencil tips racing over paper, marking pluses and minuses, balancing and writing chemical symbols. I pretty much had no idea what he was talking about or how to really solve the problem. I couldn't figure out what had happened, but chemistry was killing me. It felt like Mr. Dugan was teaching at double speed and was speaking in another language half the time. I didn't even know where to start.

It probably didn't help that instead of at least trying to figure the work out, I kept looking at the new girl, Lydia Krane. She flipped open her book and quickly found the

section that we were on. Mr. Dugan was writing problems and solutions on the board.

She looked back and forth between her book and the
board for a minute or two. I saw a flash of pink on the T-
shirt she wore under the black shirt. She looked down at
her black boots, and I could see just the edge of her face
through the black hair. She looked tense. I guessed it was
because she was so different, maybe she felt she didn't
totally belong there. I knew that feeling myself.

∽◦∾

"I hate this," Jane said.

We were at Jane's house. We were on opposite ends
of the big couch, pushing our socked feet gently back and
forth, sole to sole.

"Hate what?" I asked.

She held up the play she was reading for her English
class: *The Glass Menagerie*. I had picked a monologue from
it last year when I auditioned for *Our Town* at school. I
kind of liked Tennessee Williams. Jane, apparently,
didn't. She frowned as she turned pages, shaking her
head once in a while.

"You want a hand with that?" I asked.

She sighed heavily. "This play totally sucks. I don't
believe anyone really likes it. I think they just pretend to."

"Come on. Don't you think it's good, in an old-
fashioned, slightly corny, obvious symbolism kind of
way? What if I read some of it out loud? Maybe that'll
bring it alive?"

"Uh, no thanks. I may not be honors material, but I actually can read," she said.

"You belong in honors as much as I do. More."

"Sure."

"You do."

"I'm not exactly a genius IQ monster like you."

Neither am I, believe me. Not since we got to high school. Everything was changing, getting so much tougher. But I didn't say anything. It wouldn't do me too much good to get my girlfriend to think I wasn't as smart as she thought I was. What she didn't know wouldn't hurt her.

I pushed my feet against hers. She pushed back with equal force. I pushed harder, and she pushed harder, too.

"Hey. Did you see that new girl?" I said.

"Who, Morticia?"

"Nice."

"What about her?"

"What do you think?"

"I think she likes black."

"She does have a look."

"Well, it isn't gonna fly here, that's for sure. That heavy eyeliner? *That's* attractive. Did you see her T-shirt? It was Strawberry Shortcake."

"What's that?"

"It's like the cute little cartoon that six-year-old girls like."

"That's funny."

"It's funny? It's just weird. It's not even like the normal

goth stuff. She won't even fit in with those people."

"What, you're saying she's gonna be an outcast because she wears black clothes?"

"I'm saying she's going to be an outcast because she has a total attitude to go along with the black style. I said 'hi' to her, just to be nice, and she totally ignored me."

"Really?"

"Yup. I don't know where she's from."

"England."

"Well, whatever. Maybe she can enjoy her vampires and death and all that by herself back in merry old England. I tried."

"Her loss."

Jane pushed her feet harder against mine. I pushed back and she pushed harder, but I held on. Her left foot slipped around my right foot and dropped hard. Her heel hit me in a really, really uncomfortable place.

I bellowed.

"Oops," she said. "That was close."

"Close? Close?" I shouted. "You need glasses."

"Ha, ha," she said. She took off her glasses and came over to my side of the couch. "Poor baby," she said. She gave me a kiss, and we fooled around a little for a while before I had to go home.

❧❦

I could smell dinner as soon as I came in the front door. And that meant that I was home late.

"Sorry," I said as I unslung my backpack and took off

my coat. Mom leaned back in her chair to catch me hanging my coat on the banister. I took it off, and she kept an eye on me as I hung it in the closet.

I moved behind my older sister, Amanda, and sat at the table. Dad frowned at his watch. I said "Sorry," again.

"Let's at least try to make an effort to be home for dinner?" Dad asked.

"I had a lot of homework. I did it at Jane's. I didn't want to stop in the middle."

"So what happened with that history paper?" Dad asked.

"I got an A minus." I put some pasta on my plate.

"That's pretty good. But I thought you knew that subject cold," Dad said. He held his fork steady over his plate, like a conductor's baton.

"He wanted me to explain the entangling alliances in more detail. I didn't know enough about it." There's always just that little bit I'm missing, no matter how much I study.

"With all the history books I have? Why didn't you just ask me?" he said. Dad was a radiologist, and he was crazy about medicine, but his other great love was military history. Don't get him started on the Battle of Thermopylae or World War I air battles unless you have a long, long time to listen.

"I didn't know he wanted me to focus so much on that."

"And how did it go with that math test on identities. Did you get it back?" Mom asked.

"I got an eighty-five." I actually got a seventy-two. Math was turning out to be as big a killer as chemistry.

"Really. What did you get wrong?" she asked.

"Just a few of the problems. It was pretty hard."

"It's all about memorization," Amanda said. "You just have to learn every formula by heart and then you can just plug everything in."

"I know. I blanked on a couple. Most of the teachers let you have a sheet with every formula. You don't have to memorize them."

"Welcome to sophomore honors math B," Amanda said.

"You need to trust yourself," Mom said. "I'm sure you knew it. Maybe you just panicked a little. Got in your own way."

"Maybe." Maybe not. Maybe I'm not *that* great at math.

"What's your average in there?" Dad asked.

"About an eighty-eight, I think, give or take." Make that take, about ten or twelve. I was in the mid-seventies. At best.

"Well, you can certainly get that up, right?" Mom said.

"Sure." Definitely. If I cheat. Or have Amanda impersonate me and take all my tests.

"Great. So don't worry about it."

Right. Don't worry about it. Not much. I concentrated on trying to eat, even though I was getting a stomachache just about every time we sat down to dinner. These dinner debriefings had been happening since fourth grade. I'd always been able to give pretty much glowing and totally honest reports that they loved. But that started to change in eighth grade. That's when I began to fall behind in math and science. Then when I hit ninth grade last year, it really started to slip away from me. I had to be careful and inflate my grades a little at the dinner interrogations. Which left me having to get desperate for tests, killing myself and doing whatever it took to get those grades up before report card time. The Grand Inquisitions at dinner made me feel like I was being tested all over again. And I didn't want to fail the tests given by my parents. So I tried to eat, hoping the conversation wouldn't turn to chemistry. Hoping, in fact, that the whole conversation would just turn away from me completely.

It was like Amanda could read my mind. Just as Mom started to take a breath to talk, Amanda clapped her hands.

"Oh, yeah. So I didn't tell you about the volleyball game," she said. "It was insane."

"What happened?" Mom asked.

"We were down by ten points, and then Cheryl gets this crazy idea for a new strategy," she began. And she launched into a long, detailed account of her varsity volleyball game.

Saved.

‹∽∾›

Later, Amanda came into the bathroom while I was brushing my teeth. I took my time.

"Could you possibly hurry up?" she said.

I took a couple more scrubs and then spat in the sink.

"Finally," she said.

"Oh, wait." I put the toothbrush back in my mouth and redid my molars.

"I'm going to kill you."

I spat once more. "Hey. Gotta get those molars. You wouldn't want me to get gingivitis, would you?"

"Right now, I wouldn't care if you got leprosy. You want me to go to the bathroom with you in here?"

"I'll pass."

"Then get out," she said, and pushed me through the doorway.

I closed my bedroom door and got out my books. I worked on my English paper for about an hour. I had it polished up to where I felt I could leave it alone. At least until morning, when I knew I'd want to change some of it. I finished up my social studies, then I turned to chem.

I worked at a bunch of reaction formulas ("formul*ae*," Mom would say) and didn't get anywhere. Everyone else in my classes seemed to have a much better feel for it than I did. I had to work so much harder at it than anyone else. It had started to become clear to me when I started high school last year: the other kids in my class were just smarter than me. It was showing most in math and science classes, where

I was definitely bringing up the rear. I'd been fine before, and now I felt like I was hanging on to that bottom rung.

I didn't want to let anyone know. And no matter what, I couldn't let my parents know.

I wheeled my desk chair over to my window.

I looked up at the picture of Cloudy Boy taped onto the glass. It wasn't a picture, actually, it was an X-ray. When I was nine, I fell off my bike and hit my unhelmeted head on the curb. It bled like crazy. Mom, who is always totally calm and reasonable, had a hard time hiding that she was on the edge of hysteria, which made *me* much more nervous. Mom and Dad took me over to the ER in the hospital where Dad worked. They did a CAT scan, and I was fine. The CAT scan was all just a bunch of colors to me, and I was still shaken up by Mom being so scared, so Dad took an X-ray, too, just so he could show me I was okay. It was a profile of my head, my skull and brain all shades of white and gray. I just couldn't stop looking at it, so he let me keep the X-ray. It was totally amazing to me that this picture showed a whole other part of me that nobody else could see, not even me. It was like another kid, but it was also me. I was really fascinated with the whole idea, that there was actually a hidden, secret me.

I got up and opened my window a couple of inches. I tried to breathe in the cool air and bring some calm and sense into my body. This stuff was not too hard for me. I would definitely be able to do it. I was a good student, top-notch. I was a great guy. My parents knew it, Jane knew it, my friends knew it. Everyone knew it.

DON'T TELL

"'I'm nobody! Who are you?'"

There was a silence in the room.

"'Are you nobody, too?'"

What had I just heard? It was Ms. Wagner, of course. She took literature really, really seriously. It was like all the writers were her friends and she got personally offended if we didn't really like something we were reading.

"Come on, people. 'Are you nobody, too?' You must know that. It's Emily Dickinson, and it's one of the strongest openings I know. Listen to it: 'I'm nobody! Who are you? Are you nobody, too?' It goes on. 'Then there's a pair of us—don't tell! They'd banish us, you know.' What does that mean?"

"It's like a plan to stay alone," Tracy Horvath said. "It's an isolationist idea."

"But there are two of them," Ms. Wagner said. "Two nobodies. Does that make sense?"

"Why not?" Mark Rafferty asked. "We've got lots of nobodies in this school!" There was the laughter that he pandered for.

"Let's get back to the poem," Ms. Wagner said. "So, isn't it a paradox? If the narrator is really nobody, then does she exist? Is she zero? What's two times zero? Still zero, right?"

I had an idea that it was about two lonely people trying to connect, but being afraid of being in the spotlight or something. English and social studies were still the classes where I felt most safe. But even there, sometimes the other kids would come out with stuff I would never have come up with. Poetry made me nervous. It was too slippery. So I didn't want to say anything out loud. If I was wrong, it would have been really embarrassing. Better just to play it safe and silent. Like Emily D. said: Don't tell.

The new girl, Lydia, spoke up.

"She *feels* like nobody. It's not a paradox. It's very clear. Many people can feel like nobody."

"So Emily Dickinson felt like nobody."

"Well, maybe, maybe not. The speaker of the poem, the narrator, seems to. Whether the narrator is Dickinson herself or a persona is another story." How had I mistaken her for British? Her accent was Southern. Wow. As cultured or exotic as the British accent made her seem, when I recognized it as really being Southern, it made me think of Tennessee Williams plays, paper lanterns, and hot New Orleans nights.

"You seem to know quite a bit about this, Lydia," Ms. Wagner said. "You like poetry?"

"Not Dickinson so much anymore. I've been reading Anne Sexton."

I doubted that anybody else in the class had ever *heard* of Anne Sexton. I didn't know too much about her, but I thought I remembered that she wrote poetry about depression and that she killed herself.

"So you like emotional poetry more than intellectual poetry?" said Ms. Wagner.

"Well, of course. Isn't that what it's all about?"

Ms. Wagner nodded in agreement, smiling as if she had found a kindred spirit. She turned back to her lesson. Lydia slouched in her chair and opened up a book she always carried, a diary or something, covered with green velvet.

I watched her write. Her face went blank, like some kind of science-fiction thing where her mind drained out of her body, through her pen, and into her little book.

We were lucky to have a table in the cafeteria that was close to the window, which helped a lot when some fresh air blew in, or the cafeteria smells thankfully escaped. The thing I liked most about lunch period was it was pretty much the only time during the school day when I could see Jane. It's not like we were all touchy-feely or making out all period or anything like that. First of all, Jane was totally not into PDAs, and I guess I wasn't either, since it always seemed like it was about showing off to other people, more than about really wanting or needing it at that exact minute, in front of everybody on the planet. Plus Tim, Scott, and Nora definitely wouldn't tolerate it. We would tolerate plenty from each other, but making out at the lunch table would never cut it.

"It's fake," Tim said, peeling the bread from his sandwich. "Just like this supposed 'meat.'"

"It's not fake," Scott said. "You can tell by the color of the blood. It's totally real." Scott was addicted to tapes of Ultimate Fighting. He became insane with frustration when we said Ultimate Fighting was fake. Which, of course, made it too much fun to resist.

"Well, I agree with all the people who think it should be banned," I said, just to get him crazy.

"Banned! It's the purest legitimate sport there is!"

"Hi, I'm Scott. I'm totally gullible," Nora said. "It's not legitimate. It's fake."

Scott frowned and massaged his arms. He'd been lifting weights since the spring, and he couldn't stop feeling his new muscles, poking his chest and arms like he was testing bread that was baking.

"Could you stop fondling yourself in public?" Nora said.

"You tell him, Itsy," I said. We sometimes called her Itsy because you could almost mistake her for a fifth grader, she was so teensy. Except for her attitude, which was pretty huge.

"And Tim," she said, "would you please stop doing that with your food? You're going to make me sick."

"Look at this," Tim said. "I don't know what it is. What do you think this stuff really is?"

"It's starting to look like a crime scene," I said. "Why don't you send it out to the lab for analysis? They might want to start with carbon dating."

"I don't know exactly what that is, but it's probably a good idea," Tim said.

"Hey," Jane said. She jabbed me with a carrot stick. "You didn't tell me that the sign-up for the drama thing is going up."

"What are you talking about? I didn't know. Where did you hear that?"

"Jordan Whiting said in social studies that it's getting posted at the end of the day."

Of course. Just as I was getting excited, the name Jordan Whiting snuffed it like a bucket of snot poured on a fire. He was a year older than us, though stuck a year behind in most of his classes. He was great-looking and very comfortable onstage. It didn't matter what the play was, Jordan Paul Whiting would get the male lead.

"What did he say?" I asked.

"Just that the sheets were going up today, eighth period."

"What's the play?"

"He didn't say."

I had been bugging Mr. Lombardi to tell me what the fall play would be, but he just kept smiling mysteriously and saying in this annoying singsongy voice, "You'll see.

Soon enough, you'll see." It was driving me crazy.

"Are you allowed to try out?" Jane asked.

"I should be okay. My grades are up." I wasn't totally sure. This was a tiny bit of a sore point at home. I'd have to see if Amanda could help at all.

"Well, if you get in, I'll come see it," Nora said. Except for the winter musical, the two other plays had terrible audience attendance. Pretty much, it was mostly the families and friends of the kids in the play.

"If you want to see really good acting, I know where you can look," Tim said, and started in on Scott about the Ultimate Fighting thing. I stopped paying attention. I couldn't wait until the end of the day. I wanted to know what the play was and get my name on that sign-up list.

Jane put her hand on my knee and held it. "You're jiggling the whole table. Relax," she said.

I barely heard a word that the teachers were saying in my next two classes. Mrs. Gottlieb wrote all this stuff on the board about a Serbian assassinating Archduke Ferdinand, and I was copying it all without thinking about it. In math, Mr. Popovich put a bunch of identities on the board, and as usual, I was sending strong telepathic brain waves to him, saying, *Don't call on me, don't call on me*, while willing myself to be invisible. I had too much on my mind to struggle with the problems. I was dying to know what the play was going to be, and whether this time there might be a decent part for me.

✽✦✽

I had my books packed up before the eighth-period final bell rang, so I could get down to the auditorium fast. There was already a small crowd of the usual suspects around the closed dark brown doors. All the drama club girls were passing around a pen to each other and taking forever just to write their names on the sheet. They were in their usual gear: baggy shirts, flannel pajama-like pants, and sneakers. They were the core of the group, and theater was the focus of their lives. Acting was what they talked about all the time, onstage and off. Jane called them the DramaRamas, and she did not mean it as a compliment.

"This here is the line to sign up for the play, right?" I heard the deep Southern drawl come from my left. I hadn't even noticed her. It was the new girl, Lydia Krane.

"Uh, yeah," said Bridget Pierce. The DramaRamas weren't an especially attractive group. Bridget was probably the best-looking of the bunch, and she had a good voice. If the DramaRamas had a leader, it was her. She had the best shot at any female lead role. She raised her eyebrows and smiled at Lydia. "But you don't have to sign up for crew. You just show up. This sign-up is for actors."

"Well, that's me," Lydia said.

The DramaRamas looked at Lydia, smiled at each other and turned away from her.

"Is that a problem?" she asked.

"Nope. No problem for us," Simone Addams said over

her shoulder. The DramaRamas smiled again and made a show of looking at each other meaningfully.

I looked at Lydia Krane. Her head was turned away, away from the DramaRamas and away from me, so I couldn't see her face. But her shoulders and neck looked kind of stiff, tense.

The DramaRamas weren't that popular. But still, they were a group, and Lydia Krane was alone, a single. In group versus single, group always wins. The DramaRamas finished signing their names just so and moved away. Lydia Krane got to the sign-up sheet and started to sign. She began to scratch at the paper with the tip of her pen.

"Great." She shook her pen out and tried again, with no luck.

"Try this," I said. She turned, and there was this total anger in her look. When she saw me holding out a pen, she looked down and said, "Thanks," in a quiet voice.

As she wrote her name, her sleeve fell down to her elbow. Her arm was covered with writing in black ink: designs, crosses, isolated words like *fight* and *sweet* and *wasteland*, and words in other languages. There was also a weird A in a circle that I think was some kind of symbol that means anarchy. I was pretty sure that it was all ink from a ballpoint, like the one she handed back to me.

She walked away toward the door.

"You get your name up there all right?" Bridget Pierce said to her.

"Yeah, I managed. Thanks for the concern."

"Any time."

Jane was right: Lydia Krane was going to have a tough time. But I didn't see what she was doing to deserve it.

I looked at the paper.

Audition Sign-Up
for Autumn Play:
Hollywood Macbeth

The first name on the list was, of course, Jordan Paul Whiting. He probably got the sheet from Mr. Lombardi to hang it up, just to make sure his name was on there first. The other names were the usual crowd. I wrote my name on the list and went over to the DramaRamas.

"Any of you guys know what this play is about?" I asked.

"Nope," Simone said. "Macbeth is Shakespeare, I know that."

"But they hadn't even discovered America at that time. Or had they? What's the Hollywood part?" Bridget Pierce said.

"It doesn't make sense," another DramaRama said. "Do you get it?" she asked me.

"Not at all," I said. I looked to the doorway, and Lydia Krane was standing there by herself, looking through the glass at the rain. I went over to her.

"Hey. I'm Ethan. We have a bunch of classes together."

"Yeah. I know."

"I didn't know you were into acting," I said.

"Well, I am." She wasn't exactly making it easy to talk to her.

"I'm glad the auditions are on Monday," I said. "That means I only have this one weekend to wrack."

"Right."

"Listen. Don't worry about those girls," I said.

"What's their problem?" she said.

"I don't know. They're really into these plays, and maybe they just don't want someone new who might get one of their roles."

"So they have to give me all that attitude?"

"I don't know."

She shook her head and breathed out hard. "Whatever." She shifted her backpack and I saw a cuddly little cartoon teddy bear ear and eye peeking out from behind her black shirt.

"Is that a Care Bears T-shirt?"

"Yeah."

"I like it. It's funny."

"It is pretty funny, isn't it," she said, totally deadpan.

I smiled at her. She looked at me. Nothing. She zipped up her jacket.

"Well, anyway. Good luck," I said. Well, I tried. I turned and walked toward the doors.

"Hey. Thanks for at least talking to me," she said.

I turned back to her. "Oh. No problem. If you need help with anything . . . I mean like if you have questions about the school, or teachers, or anything, really, just let me know."

She looked at me for a second, then looked away. "Thanks. I will."

"See ya around."

"See you," she said.

☙ ❧

It was Friday night. I was with Jane, Scott, Tim, and Nora on the outside patio of Starbucks. We could have been inside, but Scott wanted room in the parking lot to practice his ultimate fighting moves against imaginary opponents. Tim and Nora looked at an eight-year-old most-boring high school yearbook that Nora had got ahold of.

"I heard Mike Napoli got suspended for smoking pot in the bathroom," Tim said.

"So what's new," Jane said. She split her chocolate-drizzled biscotti in two and gave me half.

We sat in silence for a while. I got dizzy watching Scott walk in circles, white iPod wires running from his pocket to his ears. Over and over again, he threw punches and kicks, stopped to touch his biceps and pecs, scrunched his face to the thrash blasting through his earphones, then walked in circles again, punching and kicking. I turned to watch the cars going by on Yates Street. The CVS was glowing from inside. It looked like a spaceship about to take off.

"Becky Shapiro got suspended for cursing in gym," Tim said.

"What are you, the police blotter?" Jane said.

Tim shrugged and leaned in for a closer look at the yearbook.

"So, that new girl was at the audition sign-up," I said.

"What a surprise. She's a DramaRama."

"She's not like them," I said.

"She went out for the play, right?" Jane said.

"I go out for the plays. I'm not a DramaRama."

"True, but you're a weirdo that way. You fit in with everyone."

Sure. Try, I *fake* it with everyone.

"The DramaRamas were pretty mean to her," I said.

"Why?" Tim asked.

"I don't know. Probably because they have everything set up the way they like it, and they don't want someone new coming after their parts. Plus they probably don't like her style too much."

"Hard to imagine," Jane said.

"She was wearing a Care Bears T-shirt. Isn't that funny?"

"How is that funny?" Nora asked.

"Because they're so disgustingly sweet and cutesy," I said.

"Hey," Tim said. "I used to like the Care Bears."

"You would," Nora said. "I still don't get why that

weird girl would be caught dead wearing a Care Bears T-shirt."

"It's ironic, Itsy," I said. "I think it's a riot."

"Yeah, it's hysterical," Jane said.

"What can I say? It's funny to me," I said.

"Wow. Maybe you should ask her out," Jane said. "You're so interested in her."

I looked over at her, and she did not look amused. I realized that it was probably a violation of the Rules for me to be talking about some other girl like that. I figured I'd better back off before I ended up in the doghouse. "Believe me, I'm not interested in her. Not at all." Maybe a little tiny bit. But it was definitely time to steer clear of the subject of the new girl.

"What's so bad about Care Bears?" Tim said. He kept sticking his finger into his mochaccino, trying to fish out some speck or something.

"Hi, I'm Tim," Nora said. "I can never keep up with a conversation."

So the conversation about Lydia Krane faded out, and we got back to our usual stuff. Just another night at Starbucks, killing time. Jane slouched in her chair, put her feet up on my lap, and looked at the moon.

I shivered. We wouldn't be able to hang out together outside like this too much longer. The weather was starting to turn.

NONSENSE

I got all my homework for the next week out of the way on Friday night. Then I holed up in my room for most of the weekend to prepare for the audition. I still wasn't totally sure what the play was about, but it obviously had something to do with *Macbeth*. I reread *Macbeth* twice and looked up some stuff online and in my father's books. It was a Shakespeare weekend.

"You've got to be kidding," Jane said on the phone. "You're telling me you're going to stay in all weekend doing that?"

"Exactly."

"You know you'll get a good part."

"I never get that good a part. Guys like Jordan Paul Whiting get the good parts."

"Well then how will reading *Macbeth* a billion times make any difference?"

"I don't know. Just trying to make sure I cover all my bases."

"You're really picking Shakespeare over me?"

"Just this once."

"That's not a very good boyfriend thing to do."

"I'll make it up to you. Promise."

"How?"

"It'll be a surprise."

"I'm sure."

So on Sunday, I focused on the big soliloquies, just in case that was Mr. Lombardi's plan for the audition. Late that afternoon, there was a knock on my door, and Amanda came in.

"I hear you talking to yourself in here. Are you auditioning for a play, or have you just gone crazy?"

"Both."

"What's the play?"

"I don't know. I think it has something to do with Shakespeare. This is from *Macbeth*. Listen: 'Methought I heard a voice cry "Sleep no more! Macbeth does murder sleep," the innocent sleep, sleep that knits up the ravelled sleave of care.'"

Amanda waved and made a cutting motion with her finger across her throat. "You sound like something out of Monty Python. The English accent kind of kills it."

"Oh. Really? Okay. Then let's try this. Um. Okay. 'Is this a dagger which I see before me, the handle toward my hand? Come, let me clutch thee. I have thee not, and yet I see thee still.'" I looked at her. "Better?"

"Well, now you sound like Robert De Niro in a mob movie."

"What should I do?"

"Can't you just do it the way you usually talk? Just be you?"

"Wouldn't that be weird?"

"I don't know. I don't really know anything about acting. But I wouldn't do it with an accent. That just seems kind of pretentious and bad."

Very encouraging. That wasn't going to make me at all nervous during the audition.

"Do *they* know about this?" she asked, pointing to the floor, meaning downstairs, meaning Mom and Dad.

"I didn't really mention it yet. You think I should?"

"Depends on how high your grades are."

"Pretty high."

"Then what's the problem? Why wouldn't you tell them?"

"I don't know." Of course I knew. And at dinner an hour and a half later, I was proven right.

"If you're doing well in all your classes, you can try out," Mom said.

"I am."

"Fine, then."

I could have left it at that, but I figured it might be a good idea just to be covered. "But what do you mean by 'doing well'?"

"You know what we mean, Ethan," Dad said. "Would you say you have at least a ninety average in each class?"

"Yes." No.

"Well, that should be okay."

I nodded. It wasn't quite okay. I had about an eighty-one, and slipping, in chem. But maybe I still had time to get that up higher.

"Just out of curiosity. What if I get in the play and some kind of catastrophe happens and I get lower than a ninety in a class."

"What kind of catastrophe?" Mom asked.

"Like if a safe falls out of a building and lands on my head."

"Well, then you probably couldn't be in the play anyway, could you?" Amanda said. I went along with the laughter.

"But seriously," I said. "What would happen if my grade somehow dropped?"

"Well, I guess you couldn't do the play," Mom said.

"But what if I was already cast and doing rehearsals and everything?"

"That would be unfortunate. You would have to drop out," Dad said.

"Really?"

"Of course. I think it's fine that you want to be in a play, but academic work is the priority here. School comes first."

"But what about making commitments?" Amanda said.

"He shouldn't make commitments that he can't

honor." Dad had a logical way about him that made it really hard to win arguments with him, even when you're totally right.

"You want to get into a good school, right?" he said.

I guess. "Right."

"And a top medical school, right?"

Not at all. "Right. But good colleges want you to have extracurriculars, too. Right?"

"True, but not at the expense of a strong GPA," Dad said. "Is this all hypothetical, about low grades? Is there something I need to know?"

"Not at all. Like you said, just hypothetical."

"You have good judgment, Ethan," Dad said. He carefully spread margarine on a slice of Italian bread, making sure to cover it evenly right to the edges. "You know how to set priorities. You're a sensible person, and you always do the smart thing."

The conversation turned to a discussion about the president and his latest statements about the Middle East. Add my knowledge of the subject to my interest in the subject, and the sum is a big fat zero. But they all found it fascinating.

I was a total oddball in my own family. They liked science; I liked drama. They liked CNN; I liked E! They were brilliant and successful at everything they did; I was not.

But they didn't need to know any of that. I had become expert at pretending I was like them. So they

could talk about boring politics for as long as they wanted. I could keep the interested look on my face all night.
I could keep up my act forever.

❧ ❧

Monday morning, Lydia Krane stopped me outside
our chemistry lab. "Thanks."

"For what?"

"For being nice to me on Friday."

"The girls were being obnoxious to you, and you
didn't deserve it."

"Well, that was really pretty nice, that you came
and talked to me. I thought about it all weekend."

"You did?"

"I did. So, are you ready for the audition?" I noticed
that she sounded British again, not Southern. I couldn't
think of a polite way to ask about it.

"I guess I'm ready. I just don't know, if he has us do
something from Shakespeare for the audition, I can't
decide whether to do it with an American accent or an
English one."

"I would say not to think so much about how you say
the words, just feel the emotion. If you do that, then the
accent isn't an issue."

"Sounds like you've done a little acting before," I said.

"A little. I was in a Lifetime cable movie, and I had
some small parts in some indie stuff."

"Really?"

"It's not so impressive, believe me."

"I think it is. Wow. So the DramaRamas had good reason to feel threatened."

"Who?"

"Those girls on Friday."

"DramaRamas. That's very funny."

"Let's go, please," Mr. Dugan called out the door. "We have a lot to do."

Lydia smiled at me and stepped through the door. She nodded. "Well, thanks again."

"Any time."

"I mean it. That was nice," she said. "I won't forget." She pulled her hair back from her face and smiled at me. Her teeth were as small as a little kid's, but white and perfect.

I felt my cheeks get hot.

"No need to blush," she said. She headed toward her seat.

When I got into my seat, Mr. Dugan said, "Okay, clear your desks."

Clear our desks? Why? Everyone put their books under their chairs or in their backpacks. I was completely confused.

"You're going to need the full period, so let's get rolling."

"What's this about?" I asked.

"Oh, about ten problems or so," Mr. Dugan said, grinning. He was very pleased with his humor. But not much was funny about this for me.

"How can we have a test when you didn't even tell us about it?" I asked.

"I certainly did," he said. "Chapter eight: basic stoichiometry. I announced it and reviewed for it on Friday? Where were you?"

I was right in this very seat. Thinking only about the play sign-up. And obviously not paying attention.

"So come on, Mr. Lederer," Mr. Dugan said. "Everybody is losing time, waiting for you to clear. So let's get with the program."

I cleared my desk. This material would have been really difficult for me even if I had spent all weekend studying for it. Which I hadn't. Which left me stuck up a certain creek without a paddle.

Within one minute, I had the test in front of me — ten problems — no idea what to do, and my grade dropping like a shot duck.

≈≈

"I'm sure you did fine," Jane said at lunch.

"I'm telling you, I failed."

"You're a super-genius," Scott said, imitating Wile E. Coyote. I've known Scott since we were on Little League for the one year I played. He went the sports route, and I went the book route. Scott was one of the nicest people I ever met, but he wasn't exactly smart. He was too easily impressed with people who read books. "You don't fail tests," he said. "It's impossible."

"Well, I failed this one."

"You always say you did bad, then you end up with ninety-fives or something," Nora said.

"First of all, I don't say I didn't do well unless I really believe that. I hate when people do that so they can get everyone to tell them how smart they are. And second, I'm telling you, I failed this test."

"What makes you so sure?" Jane asked.

"How about leaving half of the answers blank and the other ones being just about total nonsense?"

Nobody said anything.

"Even if I got a sixty-five, which I didn't, that would put my grade point average at seventy-four. Not going to cut it at my house."

"Oh, jeez. This is horrible," Tim said. We all turned to him. He was holding a grayish piece of bologna up between his fingers.

Nora punched him in the arm.

❧ ❧

I went to the lab just after eighth period, and Mr. Dugan was stuffing a pile of lab reports into his bag.

"Mr. Dugan, I was hoping you could help me out with something."

"What's that?"

"Well, I'm going to be totally honest. I wasn't really prepared for the test today."

"I'm sorry to hear that." He zipped up his bag.

"I was hoping you might be willing to let me take a retest."

"How would that be fair to the other students, for you to have a second chance?"

"I mean, maybe you could average the two test grades. It's just that, because I wasn't prepared, I don't think the test was really an accurate measure of what I can do."

"Actually, being prepared is part of the accurate measure of what you do. This is an honors course. We have rigorous standards and high expectations. We don't give retests. Your grade will stand."

"Okay."

"So, Ethan. Next time? Make a little more effort and remember to study."

Thanks for the tip.

❦ ❦

When I got to the auditorium after school, Lydia Krane was already there. She waved me over. "I saved a seat for you," she said. I sat down next to her. I noticed that some of the DramaRamas in the front row saw me sit with her. One of them said something to another that I couldn't hear.

"You seem way nervous," Lydia said.

"It's not about the audition. Well, it is, but also some other stuff. I have some things on my mind."

"If I were you, I'd totally focus on the audition."

Before I could answer, Lydia pointed to the stage and said, "Who is that idiot?"

"Him? That's Jordan Paul Whiting." He had come

onto the stage from somewhere behind the curtains. Several of the DramaRamas gathered at the stage apron to talk to him. He grinned at them in his charming way.

"He sure seems to think a lot of himself, doesn't he?" Lydia observed.

"He's a legend in his own mind," I said. "Actually, as you can see, he does have a fan club."

"Why?"

"Why? He's good-looking, he has money, and he drives an Escalade."

"He isn't that good-looking."

"I think his fan club would disagree. So would most of the rest of the school. And he *will* get the lead in this play."

"How do you know?"

"Because he always does." I looked at him, standing under the lights. He would always, always get the starring role. Guys like him always did.

"Maybe you'll get the lead."

"Nope. I'm forever fated to play the best friend, or the sidekick, or the little quirky character role. I'll never be center stage."

"Can I have your attention for a moment, folks?" Jordan Paul Whiting called out to the small bunch of us scattered around the auditorium. "Phil said he'll be here in a couple of minutes, and he'd like us all gathered in the first couple of rows so we can get on with the show."

"He calls the teacher by his first name?" Lydia asked.

"He believes that he's Mr. Lombardi's protégé or

something. Special professional relationship and all that."

"This Jordan seems like a real ass."

"You're a good judge of character."

Lydia and I moved up a few rows so we were close to the front when Mr. Lombardi came in, carrying a stack of papers. He leaned against the stage, and Jordan jumped down into the pit to stand near Mr. Lombardi, like his lieutenant.

"Okay, people. Good afternoon and welcome to our auditions for the fall production. This year we have a play that I'm very excited about. It's nice to see many of our talented players back again. And welcome to the new faces, as well. Our play this fall will be *Hollywood Macbeth*. 'What,' you're asking yourselves, 'is that?' It just happens to be the work that I labored over all summer. This piece is an interpretation, if you will, of one of the best of Shakespeare's tragedies, in modern times, in contemporary language. All of the good parts, with none of the filler. It's a Hollywood story about how a movie star and his wife will literally kill to make it to the top of the movie business. "

He smiled at us. He seemed to be waiting for something, but I don't think anybody knew what to say.

"It's also going to be multimedia. Since this is about Hollywood, we'll have a 'film crew' shooting and playing video during the performance as part of the story. This is very ambitious for us, and I'm working on getting us some media coverage, as well as some theatrical agents in attendance."

A bunch of people clapped. I would have bet that several kids started making plans for the 90210 zip code that they imagined would follow their being discovered in West Baring's auditorium. Not too likely.

"I have a very clear idea of what I'm looking for, so I'm hoping to make this process relatively quick and painless. Auditions will be today and tomorrow. Our cast list should be ready for you by the end of eighth period on Friday. All righty, then. Shall we? Gentlemen, you'll take a look at the monologues on these green sheets. Mesdames, you shall grace us with the words on the yellow sheets. You'll have fifteen minutes to look it over outside, and I'll start calling you in to audition. In the words of our protagonist Mike Beath, 'Let's get this trippy-trip rolling. Peace out, peace up.'"

We stared at him. The auditorium was silent until Jordan Paul started clapping, slowly. I looked over at Lydia Krane. She looked at me, shrugged, and joined all the others in applauding. I joined in, too. We took our papers and went off into our own little areas of the lobby.

I read through the monologue four times. It didn't make too much sense to me. I looked around. Everyone else was reading their monologues, their lips moving, brows rising and falling, hands gesturing awkwardly. I looked back at it and started trying to read it to myself with some kind of feeling. But I couldn't stop thinking about how badly I messed up that test. It was impossible to concentrate on the words on my sheet.

"Hey, does yours make sense to you?" It was that Southern accent. I looked up to see Lydia Krane standing over me. "The girls' scene is really weird."

"I don't know. It's pretty strange."

"Do you want to run it past me? Until one of us is called?"

"No. I think I'm going to wing it. Hey. Did you know about that chemistry test today?"

"Of course. He talked about it all period on Friday."

"Right." I'm an idiot.

"If I were you, I would forget about the test for now and concentrate on being present for this audition."

"In the moment."

"In the moment, exactly."

I guess I picked up something from all those episodes of *Inside the Actors Studio* after all.

🙰 🙰

"My audition was a reading from hell."

"Really?" Jane asked. "I doubt it."

"I stammered, I had to start again twice. I just got all caught up in the words, stumbling over them like a drunk on an obstacle course." I switched the phone to the other ear. "I totally sucked. He probably won't even let me crew for the show, for fear that I'd suck all the talent off the stage if I'm anywhere near it."

"Maybe it felt worse than it was," she said.

"Well, it felt pretty bad."

"Hang on a minute. Pit stop." I could hear the clattery

sound as Jane put the phone on the little table next to her bed. I heard her door open and I pictured her walking down the hall to the bathroom. I listened to the music she had on in her room. We stayed on the phone for hours. There were times when one of us would wolf down dinner, while the other held on, although I guess it wouldn't have been a big deal just to call the other one back if there was some interruption like needing to go pee or eat a meal.

I thought about how completely awkward all my movements felt during the audition. I moved around just to move around, no purpose or motivation for my actions. I knew I blew it, no matter how much Jane tried to reassure me.

Lydia Krane had said the same stuff to me after the auditions. "I felt like I totally embarrassed myself at an audition once, and it turned out that I ended up getting cast in a Lifetime cable movie," she'd said. "You never know." Oh, but I knew.

"Did you tell your parents about the chem test?" Jane was back.

"Not a chance."

"Aren't they going to find out sooner or later?"

"No, because I'm going to make sure I get an A on the next one."

"I'm sure you will."

I was sure, too. No matter what, I was going to ace that test.

FOG

During swim season, Jane went to school early, so we didn't walk together. When I was walking alone, I liked to take a shortcut through the woods.

There was a pond I passed that had a layer of wispy fog hanging over it on cool mornings. It was amazingly creepy and beautiful. I sat on a rock, zipped up my jacket, and looked at the fog. It floated two feet above the black water like it was alive. This was *Macbeth*; this was the world he lived in. Chilly and damp, foggy and strange. I could smell the rot of the leaves, the soggy earth, the decomposition on the bottom of the pond.

"I knew you'd be here."

I leapt off the rock and fell on the ground. I spun around and tried to catch my breath.

It was Lydia Krane.

"You scared the crap out of me!" I said. My heart was going to punch out of my chest. I felt that tingly flow of adrenaline flooding through my body like cold honey.

"Sorry. I didn't mean to," she said.

"What are you doing here?"

"I figured you might cut through here, so I thought I'd meet you. I didn't plan on giving you a heart attack."

"It's all right. I'm fine." Except for feeling embarrassed about getting startled and falling on the ground like a total spaz.

"What were you doing, sitting there on that rock?"

"Actually, I was thinking how this is like a scene from *Macbeth*."

"You're kidding. I was thinking the same thing," she said.

"Really?"

"Really."

"That's so weird," I said.

We started walking through the last stretch of woods before getting to the road behind the school. I wasn't sure, but now her accent sounded Southern again.

"Isn't the cast list going up Friday?" she asked.

"It's supposed to."

"I hope we're both in it." She reached over and squeezed my arm through my jacket.

"That would be cool."

"So what's up with all the kids in our classes?"

"What do you mean?"

"Well, they're pretty serious."

"Hey. Honors classes. They take it all totally seriously."

"They? But not you?"

"I guess I do, but not in the same way."

"They don't seem like too much fun," she said.

"They're not. I don't have that much to do with them outside of class."

"How come?"

"I don't know."

"You feel like you don't totally fit in with them?"

"Not totally."

"Yeah. Welcome to my world," she said.

We were almost out of the woods and on the road when I spoke. "There's something I've been wondering about, but didn't know how to ask you."

"That's so funny. I was about to say that to you. Wouldn't it be funny if it was the same thing?"

"That would be funny."

"Well, you go first," she said.

"Okay. I was wondering where exactly you're from."

"I'm from all around."

"Oh. Because, I don't mean this in any kind of jerky way, but I can't exactly tell what your accent is."

"Well, I change it."

"You what?"

"I change it to whatever mood I'm in. Sometimes I feel quite English," she said in the British accent. "Sometimes I'm feeling down-home Southern," she drawled. "Some of the time, I am have the Russian feeling," she said in what I guess was a Russian accent. "Depends on my mood."

"But why?"

"For fun," she said, back in the British accent. Or was it the Southern one?

I stopped walking. She stopped, too, and turned to me. The wind blew her hair across her face.

"Well, don't you worry that people will think you're a little strange?" I asked.

"I *am* a little strange."

There wasn't much I could say to that. I nodded a couple of times and headed down the hill to the school. She didn't say anything until we were right outside the doors.

"Hey. I didn't get to ask my question," she said.

"Right. Go ahead."

"Do you have a girlfriend?"

"Do I what?"

"I said, do you have a girlfriend or anything?"

"Oh. Well, yes." Of course I heard her the first time. And I know it's totally damning of me to have hesitated, to have stalled before answering. I tried to shrug it off and ignore what I was doing, but the truth is that I didn't give a straight answer right out of the gate. Bad.

"But things aren't going so well with her, I guess," she said.

"Why do you say that?"

"Well, you just confirmed it. You didn't deny it; you just asked why I asked."

"No. Things are fine. Everything is good," I said.

"Don't worry. You don't have to turn all red. I was just curious." She yanked on the steel handle and held the door open for me. I reached behind her and held it for her. We went through together.

∾ ∾

I waited with Tim outside the gym after second period until Jane came out. Her hair was still wet from swim practice, dark curls and corkscrews leaving a darker wet spot where they touched the shoulders of her T-shirt. She smiled when she saw me and squeezed my wrist for a second.

"You're in a good mood," I said.

"I'm feeling good. My times are getting better for the relay."

"They're probably going to pick you to be captain next year," I said.

"Doubt it. Either of you guys have any gum?"

Tim took a pack out of his front pocket and two more out of his backpack. Tim always had at least three types of gum. Jane raised her eyebrows at one of them. "Strawberry Sundae?"

"It's new," Tim said.

"Why would you even buy that?" I asked.

"It didn't turn out to be as good as it sounded. But try it."

"No thanks," Jane said, picking basic old Trident. We walked her to class. Tim and I had third-period classes near each other so we headed to the B wing fast before the bell rang.

"You're lucky," he said.

"Why?"

"Why? You have an awesome girlfriend. You're like super-genius. You have a normal family. You've got it all."

I nodded. Tim's parents were totally overprotective, probably still tucked him in at night. He had trouble in every subject except computers and lunch. And he'd never even come close to kissing a girl. My life probably did seem great to Tim. He was right.

What did I have to worry about?

❧ ❧

"Some of you got quite a lot of these wrong," Mr. Dugan said. He moved around the room passing back the chem tests. He folded each paper in half and whipped it out with a snap to each kid.

He arrived in front of me and stared at my test for a couple of seconds before he snapped it to me. It said:

45 Failing grade! ! !
See me after class

Suddenly my stomach hurt.

"There is some good news," he said after he handed back the last paper. "Next week, we'll be having our objective test on everything we've covered so far. Mols and reactions, including single and double replacement, synthesis, and decomposition reactions. This will be the final test for the marking period. So those of you who need it will have a chance to redeem yourselves."

Not too likely for me.

When the bell rang, I took a long time to gather my stuff up so the class would all leave and I wouldn't have to talk to Mr. Dugan in front of them. Lydia Krane stayed at the door until she caught my eye. I shook my head and mouthed "Go ahead" to her. When everyone was gone, I went over to Mr. Dugan.

"You didn't quite dazzle me on that test, Mr. Lederer."

I nodded.

"The only reason you got a forty-five was that I felt you should get some points for at least trying to solve some of the problems. It was pretty obvious, though, that you didn't really know how to approach them. All in all, not very impressive. Do you have anything to say?"

Other than, You're a sadistic asshole? "Not really."

"I think you would agree that you're not quite cutting it in honors chemistry."

The ramifications of what he was saying were going to make me think about a whole bunch of things that were better off left unthought. "Well, I had one bad day, right? I mean, that doesn't mean that we have to do anything, you know, permanent, does it?"

"I think it's more than one bad day. Let's be honest. You're not quite honors chemistry level, are you?"

"I can do it."

"Well, we'll see."

"What do you mean?"

"I mean that if you don't get a stellar grade on the objective test, I'm going to recommend that you be switched to a class level more suited to your abilities."

"My parents would be . . . very upset if I got moved out of honors chem."

"That may be, but it isn't really my problem, is it? I do have the other seventeen students to consider, and we can't progress at the rate we need to if we have dead weight in here."

I wasn't sure if I'd heard right. Did he really just call me dead weight? Is that what he said?

"I don't mean that in a harsh way," he said. "I hope you take it in the spirit in which it was intended."

"I think I understand you perfectly."

"Excellent. So we'll see what happens on the objective test."

As I walked out, I wondered if anyone would have suspected me if I stabbed Mr. Dugan to death with his stupid pointer. Or if anyone would be sorry about it.

❧❧

I worried like crazy about the chem objective test. It was like this dark cloud, and whenever I would forget about it for a little while, it seemed like something would immediately remind me. Even a TV commercial about car mufflers—when the actor playing a garage owner said, "It just doesn't add up, pal," the idea of something adding up made me think of chem. And thinking of chemistry meant thinking about my impending doom. I couldn't even look forward to the posting of the cast for the play, because it only reminded me of how there was no way in the world I would be allowed to be in it if I got thrown out of honors chem. I wasn't even totally sure that my parents wouldn't consider moving to another state and adopting new identities to avoid the shame and disgrace they were going to suffer because of me.

Jane kept asking me what was wrong, but there was no way I could tell her that I was going to get booted out of honors chem. She admired me too much, and I wasn't about to kill that.

❧❧

Lydia Krane pulled me aside after class eighth period on Friday.

"I think the cast list is supposed to go up. Let's go see."

All the excitement was sucked out of going to see the cast posting. I almost hoped I didn't get a part, since that would mean a bigger disappointment when I wouldn't be allowed to take it. Still, Lydia was really excited to go, and she gripped my arm as she pulled me through the halls. I felt kind of awkward, because if Jane saw Lydia holding me like that, she wouldn't be too happy about it.

Of course, the DramaRamas were gathered around the cast list. They were snarking about something. I heard one of them say, "Who *is* she, anyways?" We got a bunch of dirty looks when they saw us trying to peer over their shoulders, but they got out of our way and moved down the hall.

The first lines of the list were:

CAST for *Hollywood Macbeth*

Mike Beath	Jordan Paul Whiting
Lei-Dee	Lydia Krane
Mark Duffy	Ethan Lederer
Ben Kwo	Steven Chen
Three Ingénues	Bridget Pierce
	Simone Addams
	Kathy Michaels

"Wow," Lydia said. "Seems like we got us some big parts." She was in the Southern accent this time.

"Yeah. Congratulations. You got the female lead. Looks like you'll be spending a lot of time with the famous Jordan Paul Whiting."

"What a thrill. I wish you'd got the male lead."

"Well, I probably won't even get to play this part," I said.

"Why not?"

"It's this thing with my parents. If I don't make certain grades, they won't let me do the play."

"Why?"

"It's a long story."

"I have time. Are you walking home?"

≈ ≈

We stopped by the pond. It wasn't foggy this time. It had all burned off, or floated away, or whatever it is that happens to fog when it clears. It was quiet, except for the sound of some birds calling to each other.

"So what's this complicated reason why you can't be in the play?" she asked.

"Because. I have to keep up the image."

"What image?" She dug the toe of her boot in the dirt and kicked some of it up onto my sneaker. I kicked a little back at her boot.

I looked at her. She was the only person around who didn't know me since I was a little kid. It had never occurred to me that there would be anybody I could tell about how I really felt. And I realized how much I really wanted to tell someone, how badly I wanted to tell Lydia. "See, my parents, my friends, my sister, my teachers. All of them think I'm so smart. My mom went to Columbia. My dad went to Yale—undergrad *and* medical school. My sister is definitely going to get accepted early decision to Harvard. I'm just not in their league."

"Why don't you tell your parents that you can't do it?"

"You don't understand. My parents think I'm like my sister and like them. I'm not. It's like that song from *Sesame Street:* 'One of these things is not like the others, One of these things just doesn't belong. . . .'"

"Ha. Tell me about it." She smiled, and I knew she understood what I meant. I wasn't sure why I was telling her all this personal stuff. Maybe it was just because it was so easy to talk to her. Or maybe I felt she'd under-stand me. Whatever it was, I told her things I'd never said out loud before.

"No matter how hard I try, I just won't ever be as smart as them, as good as them. They want me to be total-ly interested in school and academics and be this perfect kid heading for great things."

"But you're not?"

"Not even close. I'm just really good at faking it."

"So I guess you *are* a pretty good actor."

"I'm doing it all the time, twenty-four/seven. Acting like I'm a good student, good son, good everything. Acting like it comes easy to me. But it's a real struggle. I feel like a total fraud half the time."

"So, does your girlfriend know about all this? That you're this big fraud?"

For some reason, I got uncomfortable whenever Lydia mentioned Jane. "No. She also thinks I'm really smart."

"I can understand. I know what it's like to pretend to be somebody you're not. But I do it for kicks. You made a big mistake."

"What?"

"You picked a role that's no fun."

"I didn't pick it."

"Well, you agreed to play it. And it's no fun playing the good boy. Especially when you're not."

"Not what?"

"Not a good boy."

I didn't say anything. It was this weird feeling, like she knew things about me that nobody could have told her, that she couldn't possibly know.

"I'm not who anyone thinks I am," I said.

"So who are you?"

"What do you mean?"

"If you're not who they think you are, then the big question is: Who *are* you?"

"I don't even know how to answer that question. Who am I? Can *anyone* answer that?"

"I think it's kind of the key to everything. I think about that question all the time."

"Have you found the answer?"

She smiled. "Still working on it. But the big trick is, you can't be afraid to find out."

I thought about what she said, and then suddenly, something became clear to me. "Maybe I am a little scared. To find out."

"You know what? I feel like I know you better than you know yourself. And guess what? I don't think you should be scared. You're gonna like what you find out when you find out who you really are."

How did she know so much? How did I get so lucky to meet someone as cool and smart and interesting as her? And how did she know me so well? I was so filled with emotion that it felt like I couldn't even swallow or I might start crying. I looked away.

"Let me guess," she said. "You get all emotional at

times, like now. And they just don't get it. So you wonder, What am I doing in this family? Is this my life?"

She tossed her hair. I noticed for the first time how her eyes were this deep, dark blue. They were kind of breathtaking, the way she was looking at me.

"How do you know me so well?" I asked. "Did I see you on the commercial for Psychic Buddies Hotline?"

"I know you so well because we're totally alike," she said. "Kindred spirits."

"We are," I said. I meant it like a question, but it came out sounding like a fact.

She grabbed my hand and held it. "I'd hate for you to have to drop out of the play. You've been a real friend to me since I came. The only one, in fact. I'm going to do whatever I can to help you with all this."

"Thanks." I got that guilty feeling again, letting her hold my hand like that. I wouldn't have wanted Jane to see this. But I didn't want to seem like I was making a big deal of it and pull away. And the honest truth was that it felt pretty good.

⁓ ⁓

Since I wouldn't go out on the weekend, Jane came over. She had wanted to go to a movie or something, anything, but I had to stay home and work.

"How are you, Jane?" my mom asked.

"Fine. How are you? Oh, I gave my mother that article you sent her. She said thanks."

"Let her know there's another migraine medication

that's about to be approved. I'll let her know when we get more information."

"Thanks. I will."

"All right," I said. "I'm going up to study if you two are gonna talk all day."

"I'm coming," Jane said. She and Mom exchanged smiles. My parents loved Jane. They overlooked the fact that she wasn't in honors classes. She was honest, hard-working, friendly, and safe, which were all qualities they valued. They knew she wasn't about to lead me into a life of drug use, criminal acts, or worse, academic mediocrity.

We studied for about an hour when Dad called up the stairs that they were going out to do some food shopping.

Jane and I were on my bed, and Jane grabbed my foot.

"What?" I said. I looked over my book.

"Stop jiggling. You're so jumpy."

"I'm having a hard time with this."

"I can't believe you're worried about your objective test. You're gonna ace it, as usual," Jane said.

"I guess." Not.

"I'm not worried about you."

"And there's other stuff. Dugan thinks I'm not honors chem material."

"He's crazy," she said.

"Well, that's what he thinks, and he's set to dump me. He wants me out. And then I'm out of the play, too. The only way I stay is if I prove him wrong and do well. I'm going to have to kill on this test."

"You will. I have total confidence in you." She squeezed my foot. She pulled my sock off and threw it at me.

"You're in trouble," I said, and jumped on her, tickling her ribs. When she tickled me back, my academic worries were put on deck for a while as other things came to my mind. We messed around for a while, but only a little. It was good, but then Jane put the brakes on at the usual point. Jane set the limits, and as always, I didn't push them.

෴ ෴

I studied my butt off until twelve-thirty in the morning, but I had to face the fact that I wasn't getting anywhere.

I knew when I was just spinning my wheels and it was time to move on to Plan B, the alternate approach to preparing for my test. I thought about how it was pretty interesting that Lydia Krane had made the comment about me not really being the good boy I pretended to be. She knew me pretty well. Better than Jane did.

Give me a piece of paper the size of a postage stamp and a black Bic fine-point pen, and I guarantee I can fit an outline of the U.S. Constitution on one side, and a list of all the presidents and their terms on the other. I can fit the phylum, genus, and species of half the animals on land and sea. I know, because I've done it.

So writing a nearly microscopic version of the entire Periodic Table of the Elements, complete with atomic numbers, weights, and electron configurations, was no sweat at all.

I was expert at writing these notes, and I was expert at concealing them during the test. I was expert at being careful when I looked at them so it didn't look like I was checking them.

During the test, it occurred to me that I could use this feeling of being expert and accomplished at subterfuge if I ever played a master criminal. I was thinking about how amazing it was that I was getting away with it and that I would very possibly ace the test, and rescue my grade. I was thinking about how I had gotten everything back on track. I was thinking about it right up to the moment I felt Mr. Dugan grab my wrist, catching me red-handed.

BUSTED

When I was nine, there was a store in town that sold everything from vitamins to clothing to toys. They had these plastic rings, with the faces of famous monsters like Frankenstein and the Wolfman on them. I thought they were amazingly cool, but ridiculously overpriced at $1.50 each. So my reasoning was that, since these rings were unreasonably expensive, I had every right to steal them. In my nine-year-old mind, I was protesting against the unfair pricing of these rings, as well as all other unjust pricing practices that were keeping important items out of the hands of deserving consumers everywhere. Important items like cars, refrigerators, food, and, of course, plastic monster rings.

My plan was brilliant in its simplicity. It was a rainy Sunday. Scott, who was also a fan of monsters, was my partner and would be wearing a raincoat with big pockets, just like I was. One of us would be around the counter, asking questions about some of the items up front. The clerk would be distracted and not notice that the other kid who was examining the plastic monster rings was not, in fact, putting them back on the rack as it appeared, but was putting them directly into his large raincoat pockets.

The plan was altered when Scott stupidly told another kid, Derek Di Maio, about our plan. Derek wanted in, and, against my better judgment, I agreed. He could be used as another distraction.

I was astonished at how easy it was. My pockets were filled with cool plastic monster rings, as were the pockets of the members of my little crime ring. Thieving is tiring work, so we headed back to my house for lunch. Mom came into my room as the three us were sitting on my bed, examining our loot. She asked where we got all that stuff. Thinking quickly, I said that Derek bought them for us. She nodded and told us that our grilled cheese sandwiches were ready.

After lunch, we plotted about all the other things we were going to steal. We went back to the drugstore and loaded up on loose candy from bins. I gave the secret signal to leave, a double sneeze followed by a cough, and headed slowly and oh so casually to the door. Derek had left a minute or so earlier, and he came running up to me and Scott. His eyes were wide. "Ethan, your parents are coming down the street, and they look really mad." In a panic, I ran around to the loading dock and actually tried to hide behind a Dumpster.

It turned out that my mom had happened to speak to Derek's mother and mentioned how generous it was for him to buy us all that stuff. Derek's mother was confused:

Derek didn't have any money with him. That's how my criminal master plan was undone.

After being forced to return the items and apologize to the store owners, I faced my parents for the lecture in our living room. Mom looked like she was going to cry.

"Didn't we raise you to be honest?" Dad asked. "Didn't we teach you about ethics and morals? How could you do this?"

Mom shook her head and said those magic words that can just about disintegrate a kid: "We thought we could trust you."

So I haven't done anything bad since then. Other than lying a little about my grades, and then cheating on some tests. But I never got caught.

And so I had gained back their trust and respect. My dishonorable activity had been excused and all but forgotten since the shoplifting incident. My probation was long over, my criminal record expunged and clean as a whistle.

"Here's what's going to happen," Mr. Dugan said. "I'm going to send you to the office now with this note. I have one more class after this period, after which I will call your parents and tell them about this." He waved my tiny square of cheat notes in front of me, as if it were a much larger sheet of paper. "I'll explain to them that you'll appear before the Student Court, which will most certainly result in a two-week suspension. In a case of cheating, it is my prerogative to give you a failing grade for the marking period. And, of course, you will be removed from honors chemistry and placed on probation for all other classes you may be in."

"Mr. Dugan, I don't—"

"I don't want to hear it," he said. "There is nothing you can say or do to change it at this point." He signed the note to the principal. "You know, I had your sister for honors chemistry two years ago. She was an outstanding student and an exceptional person besides. You're obviously nothing like her."

I didn't say anything. I just tried to keep my breathing calm and steady. He handed me the note and a pass to the main office.

"I wouldn't want to be you when your parents find out about this," he said.

I didn't want to be me, either.

Of course, I didn't go to the office. That was technically a cut, which I never did. But in the grand scheme of things, worrying about getting a day of detention for cutting at this point was like worrying about a mosquito bite that was right next to a sucking chest wound.

I went to the library and found a corner carrel far away from everything. Going to Student Court meant that everyone in school would know about it. And the suspension. Mom and Dad would love that. Almost as much as they would love my getting booted out of honors. Oh, and add the academic probation in my other classes. And all my teachers would know why.

Mom and Dad would look at me as a cheater. And what was Jane going to think? How could she ever look at me the same way again? She'd think I was a fraud and a loser. Which wasn't too far from the truth.

"Hey." I jumped. It was Lydia.

"How come you always just appear out of the blue?" I asked her.

"It's not out of the blue. I was looking for you." She pulled over a chair and squished into the carrel with me. "What happened?"

"Well. I cheated on the chem test."

"Really? I knew there was a bad-boy side to you."

"It's not funny."

"Well, it's not like you killed somebody or anything. Okay, so what's going to happen to you?"

"I'm going to be suspended; I'm going to fail chem for the marking period, which, of course, will completely trash my entire GPA. I'm going to get thrown out of honors chem, get put on academic probation."

"Is that all?"

"Is that all? No, it's not. I'll get a reputation as a cheat. All the kids in my classes will know. The teachers will know." The more I thought about it, the worse it was. "Ms. Wagner is going to look at me as a cheater. Let's not forget Mr. Lombardi. Not that it matters, because being in the play is history. I also get to deal with my parents, who just won't get over this. I'll never live it down."

"Did you ask Dugan for another chance?"

"Are you kidding? He wouldn't even listen to me. He's going for the most severe consequences."

"What a total jerk."

"He *is* a jerk, but it's all my own fault. I cheated and I got busted. I'm cooked." I felt like puking.

Lydia looked away from me for a moment.

"Serves me right," I said. "I did it just a few times in middle school. Only when I was really desperate. But since ninth grade, it's like I've had to do it more and more. I've done it so much that I don't even feel so guilty anymore."

Lydia made a face. "So what. Guilt is stupid."

"Guilt is stupid?"

"Yeah. It's stupid. And it's not going to help you get out of this, anyway."

"There's no way out. I cheated, and now I'm getting nailed. I guess I deserve it."

"Okay, but Dugan is acting like you committed the crime of the century. He's taking it way too far. There has to be a way to get him to leave you alone."

"You don't know him. He's totally serious about chemistry and honors classes and stuff like that. He's head of the Honor Society, and he doesn't mess around about anything."

She thought for a while. Then, after a minute, she smiled. "I can fix this," she said.

"How?"

"I bet if I talk to him, he'll let it go."

"You're crazy."

"Come on." She took my hand and pulled me along.

"Wait. I can't go back there."

"You want to get out of this or not?"

We got to the chem lab just as the bell for last period rang. The kids filed out, and the halls got loud. Lydia leaned into the lab to see if all the kids had left.

"Wait here," Lydia said to me.

"What are you going to say?"

"Just wait here for now."

Lydia went inside and pulled the door almost closed. I waited outside. She had personality, and she was pretty smart, but I knew there was no way she could talk Mr. Dugan out of taking action against me. He said he thought I didn't belong in honors, and I had proved him right. He liked being right.

"Hey!" I heard Lydia call out. "Hey," she called again.

I went in.

Mr. Dugan was standing behind his desk, facing Lydia, who was standing in the narrow space between him and the blackboard. Mr. Dugan looked at me. His face was red.

"You see this, Ethan?" Lydia said to me, no accent at all. Just scary serious.

"See this?" I said.

"Yes. You're a witness. I came in here to talk to Mr. Dugan about how he's accusing you of cheating and about how it was a misunderstanding and all. And then he tried to touch me."

"I did not!" Mr. Dugan said, his voice cracking.

"Yes, you did! Ethan, he tried to kiss me and feel me up."

"This is ridiculous," Mr. Dugan said. His face was the color of a red Sharpie.

"Don't lie. All I wanted to do was clear up a misunderstanding about my friend and then you go and do this."

"This is crazy."

"I have a witness. But even if I didn't, if I go ahead and tell about this, your teaching career is finished. That is, if you don't go to jail," Lydia said. Mr. Dugan got himself away from Lydia and ended up between us, in the corner.

"This is going to be one big scandal," she said. "Trying to molest a student. Oh, my God. My mother is going to go ballistic. She'll go right to the district attorney and then to the newspapers. And people will look at me as the girl that the creepy chemistry teacher fondled."

There were actual tears filling her eyes.

Mr. Dugan's mouth moved, but he couldn't get any sound to come out.

"Hold on," I said. I couldn't get my mind around what was happening.

"Unless," Lydia said. "Unless I go and try to be the understanding person my mom taught me to be. People make mistakes, she always said. So I'm thinking if you overlook the whole mistake about Ethan, I might be able to overlook the mistake you made with me."

"You think you can get away with this? Are you actually trying to blackmail me?" Mr. Dugan shook his head slowly. "I can't believe you're doing this."

"I'm not doing anything except offering you a chance to get out of a lot of trouble, Mr. Dugan. If you don't want it, and you'd rather take your chances with the school board and the prosecutors and the press, that's your choice."

Mr. Dugan glared at me.

"So what's it gonna be?" Lydia said.

Mr. Dugan looked at her, and his shoulders slumped. "I don't want trouble," he said in a very quiet voice.

"And I'll take that little piece of paper—those study notes—that you took from Ethan, too. You won't be needing that."

When we got outside into the hallway, I touched Lydia's arm and stopped her.

"What just happened?"

"What just happened was I saved your butt," she said. She rolled the paper with my cheat notes into a tiny ball. "Just like I promised."

THAT KIND OF GUY

"I'll get right to the point. This is really about lust. However you cut it, it's about lust. Lust for power, lust for social position, lust for love. When we act on our emotions, we do things we never would have believed possible. We can perform acts of great courage and acts of vile cowardice. We can stand honorable in the face of temptation, or we can betray all of our morals in a moment of passion. That's what this is about, and that's what we're here for. Acting. Passion. And hopefully, along the way, we'll learn a thing or two about ourselves."

Call me sentimental, but this kind of stuff got to me. That's why I liked Mr. Lombardi so much. He seemed like this mild, ordinary-looking guy, kind of a nerdy type that you'd just pass on the street without thinking anything. But inside, he had this passion, these ideas. He was a poet, really, a guy who believed in things that matter.

I looked at the other kids sitting on the folding chairs we had set up on the stage. The DramaRamas all had expressions of concentration and deep thought on their faces. Jordan Paul Whiting was stroking his chin, smiling knowingly, and nodding. All the other kids in the cast and the crew were just waiting for the action to start, trying not to stare at the pile of scripts. I wasn't sure that any of them really believed what Mr. Lombardi was talking about.

But Lydia Krane got it. She looked over at me. We nodded to each other a couple of times.

Nobody else in the auditorium knew that I shouldn't have even been there. That day Mr. Dugan had totally avoided looking me in the eye. Which was all right with me, since I would have found it hard to look him in the eye, too. But I slowly peeped at my test when he gave it back and I was pretty astonished to see an A written on top. I looked up at him, but his back was to me. I would have taken the F on the objective test without complaint, just as long as he didn't nail me to the wall for cheating. Obviously, I didn't deserve an A by any kind of normal reasoning.

"This is about a basically good man who is brought down by a tragic flaw," Mr. Lombardi said. "Don't be fooled into thinking that he's all good and it's all her fault that he's driven by her to do these horrible acts. That would not be tragedy, it would be bathos. Melodrama."

I looked over at Lydia. Her face was the picture of calm. It was so weird, how I had all these mixed feelings about her. Like the whole thing that she did with Mr. Dugan. On the one hand, it was pretty impressive how she took control of the situation. On the other hand, it was a little bit scary.

"The tragedy is that his own flaws ultimately cause his downfall. What those flaws are, I will leave to you to discover as we explore this dark, dark tale together. So!" He clapped, suddenly almost cheerful. "Let's get you the scripts and get to work."

He split a large pile of scripts in two and passed them both ways around the circle.

"In short, I've kept the basic plot of *Macbeth* and taken the liberty of giving it a new setting. Our story of ambition, lust, and power run amuck takes place on the Hollywood set of an action movie. If you want a story about power, lust, and betrayal, you can find no better setting than Hollywood. We follow our protagonist, actor Mike Beath, 'rhymes with death,' in his words, as he struggles to reach the top of the Hollywood star list. Jordan Paul will play this part. Mike Beath is 'encouraged,' shall we say, by his fourth wife, former starlet Lei-Dee, played by Lydia Krane. His rival is another actor named Mark Duffy, who vows to destroy Mr. Beath. Ethan Lederer is our Duffy. And you'll meet all the others as we read through. This year we have a very talented cast and crew. So now that you all have your scripts, let's do our first read-through together."

We all opened our scripts.

"One more thing," Mr. Lombardi said. "You want to be actors. You're going to analyze your characters, their personalities. Their motivations, their actions. Why does he do this? What was her childhood like? That's fine. You have to understand the character you're playing. But first, you have to understand yourself. You have to find that part of the character that's part of you. You can't play a character that isn't in you. Not without it being a disaster. So before you try to know the person you're playing, you have to answer the more important question: How well do *you* know *yourself*?"

※※

We were walking by the pond, on the way home. Lydia stopped and picked up a rock at her feet. She threw it into the pond. She had a pretty good arm. "You know, you were right about that guy, John Paul."

"Jordan Paul," I said.

"Whatever. He's not very good at all."

"I told you," I said.

I picked up a rock myself and was about to throw it in after hers, but I realized there was a chance I couldn't throw it as far as she had, and that would frankly be a little bit embarrassing. So I tossed it up and down in my hands a few times, then picked up two more stones that were about the same size and started juggling them.

"Hey," she said. "That's pretty good."

"No big deal." No big deal after countless hours of practice, day and night, when I was ten, driving my family crazy, until every round piece of fruit in the house was mushy and bruised from my training.

"That part should have gone to you," she said.

"My part's pretty big. I'm fine with it."

"Still."

I was concentrating on my juggling. She snatched one of the rocks I was juggling right out of the air. I was able to keep it going for a couple of seconds more, before I lost my rhythm and the other rocks fell. We sat by the pond.

"I like this place," she said.

"It's a good place to think. It's quiet. I come here a lot."

"Peaceful."

I nodded. We sat without saying anything for a while. I was thinking about the rehearsal. "Something he said kind of hit a chord with me," I said.

"Lombardi?"

"Yeah. That thing about how you can't really play a part that's not in you. I don't know why, but that's really sticking with me."

"Sure. It's because the good boy honest honors student character you play feels bad because it's not really in you."

"Maybe."

"Maybe?"

"Okay, definitely." It suddenly made sense.

"So what can you do about it?"

I tossed a stone in the pond. "I guess either I find that part inside me, or I find a new character."

Lydia nodded and threw a rock in the water. The ripples from her stone moved toward the ripples I made until they met and washed each other away.

✐✐

"Jane called you three times," Amanda said when I got home. "Call her back."

"I'll call her after I eat something."

"No, call her now. She called three times. Call her back."

"I don't know why she had to keep calling when she knew I was working on the play." I opened the refrigerator.

"I know you like to act, but don't act like a jerk. Don't be *that* boyfriend, don't be *that* guy." Amanda grabbed my arm, pulled me out of the refrigerator, and closed it.

"Who is 'that' guy?" I opened the pantry cabinet.

"It's the one who says his girlfriend is nagging him, the one who says he doesn't want to be fenced in or tied down or whatever. The one who treats his girlfriend like an obligation that he tolerates. The one who says he needs freedom, or that he needs to see other people, 'just to make sure that this is real.' That guy. Don't be that guy. You never were before. Don't start now."

"Still angry about Robert, huh?" I said. I just managed to snag a package of Pop-Tarts before Amanda shut the pantry door, barely missing my fingers.

"This has nothing to do with him. But if you really want to be a jerky guy who treats girls like crap, go ahead and keep her waiting for your phone call. I don't really care what you do."

She went upstairs, leaving me standing there with that *What'd I do?* feeling that I seemed to be getting more and more often. "Sorr-*eee!*" I called up the stairway, realizing immediately how insincere and childish I sounded.

"I told you that I had rehearsal," I said to Jane on the phone a few minutes later. "You didn't have to keep calling."

"Why didn't you call me from your cell phone when you were walking home?"

Somehow, I got the feeling that saying I was walking with Lydia would only get me deeper into the doghouse. "It's dead. I have to charge the battery."

"Oh. That's why I got your voice mail. I called your cell before I called your house."

"Well, that's why." Actually, probably my not having it turned on was the real reason. "What's going on?" I said.

"Nothing. Just flipping through the channels and hanging around. How was practice?"

It always bothered me that she called it *practice*, like I was crashing helmets in football. But it seemed obnoxious and picky to keep correcting her by calling it *rehearsal*, so I just let it go. "It was good."

"That's good." There was a pause. "What are you going to do now?"

"I'll just eat something and then try to get my homework done."

"Hey. Nora may have mono."

"That's pretty hard to believe. How would she have gotten it? Wait, did she actually kiss someone? Should I call the newspapers?"

"You know that's a myth. You can get it from breathing the same air as someone who has it. I think."

"Well, that's too bad. When will she know if she has it?"

"I don't know. Soon, I guess. So . . ." she kind of trailed off.

"What?"

"Nothing. Never mind."

I hated this kind of thing, when someone said, By the way, oh, never mind, it's nothing, trying to get you all curious so you'd beg them to say what they wanted to say. I didn't say anything.

"So," she finally said. "Like, who do you hang around with at the play practice?"

"Whoever's there."

"What about that Lydia girl?" This was what I thought she was getting at.

"She's there."

"You hang around with her?"

"Well, she's there. What am I supposed to do, pretend she's not?"

"Why are you getting all defensive?"

"I'm not. I'm just saying. She's there."

"She got a big part, right? Is she that good?"

"She's okay." Actually, she was a whole lot better than okay. She was great. I could understand how she got cast in real movies. She really knew how to get into her character. She seemed like a totally different person onstage.

She didn't speak in either the British accent or the Southern accent, or any other accent. When she spoke, it changed the whole level of the rehearsal. It was like all the rest of us were all Acting with a capital A, while she was actually becoming the character.

"You still there?" Jane said.

"I'm here." I talked with her for a while about basic stuff, like how her sick grandmother was doing, how she did on a history test she got back, how Scott was trying to get out of going on vacation with his family so he could stay home by himself. After a while, I was able to tell her that I had to get to my homework.

I had trouble falling asleep that night. I would admit that my tone might have been a little harsh with Jane on the phone before, but she was really acting a little annoying. Okay, so maybe I wasn't being totally and completely honest about Lydia. But if Jane was going to go accusing me of things I wasn't even doing, really, then I felt I had the right not to have to tell her every little thing about my hanging out with Lydia.

I threw my blanket off me, down to the foot of the bed.

The truth was that I found myself thinking about Lydia quite a lot. In class, I'd look over at her and wonder what she was thinking. At rehearsal, I waited for her scenes to come up so I could watch her move across the stage as Mr. Lombardi blocked stuff out. And when I was home, I wondered what she was doing. Maybe the worst part was that when I was with Jane, or talking to her, I was thinking about Lydia. Even though nothing had happened, I knew that it was a betrayal of Jane for me to think about Lydia so much.

As Amanda said, I didn't want to be that guy. But I was doing stuff that made me wonder a little bit. What kind of guy was I, anyway?

TRANSPARENT

"Hey," Lydia said. "I was looking for you." She grabbed my arm and held it. We were in the hallway, and swarms of kids were passing us. I was always stuck between liking when Lydia touched me and feeling nervous that Jane might see us and read something into it. "Come over to my house today after school."

"What about rehearsal?"

"Canceled. There's a note on the auditorium door. Come over and we can rehearse together?"

"Rehearse at your house?"

"Yeah."

"You and me?"

"Yeah. Is that a problem?"

Good question. Why should rehearsing be a problem, even if it was just the two of us? I was sure I could learn a lot from her. But on the other hand, Jane was acting pretty eager to spend time with me, sounding like she felt a little neglected, and I'd better use this time to make things up to her a little.

"What are you thinking about?" Lydia asked.

"I'm just thinking about if I can do it."

"Ah. Maybe you need to check with your wife first."

"What?"

"If you have to call her to get *permission* . . ."

"I don't need to get permission from her. I'll meet you out back after school."

"Sounds good," she said.

≈ ≈

To get to Lydia's house, you take a left after the pond, instead of a right, which is how you get to my house. We walked on the minibike trail, trying to avoid the deep ruts left by tires.

She lived in the part of town where the houses were smaller and closer together. She turned off the sidewalk onto a cement walkway that was badly cracked and uneven, like some large animal had burrowed its way underneath it. The house looked like it could use a paint job. Lydia pushed the front door open, which made a sound like a kitten being squeezed.

The living room was mostly dark, except for a little light that came through yellow shades. The TV was on, playing some old movie that nobody was watching. The couch and the two chairs looked worn out, tired.

"You want something to eat?" Lydia asked. She opened the refrigerator, and I was hit with the smell of leftover Chinese food.

"I'm good," I said. She pulled out some cans of soda and shut the refrigerator.

"Be right back," she said. She went around a corner and shut a door—a bathroom, I guessed.

I walked closer to the TV and tried to figure out what the movie was. It was in black and white, and the guy was good-looking in that rugged old Hollywood way.

"Who the hell are you?"

I just about jumped out of my skin. There was a guy sunk into the couch who I hadn't seen. He looked to be in his early twenties. He was tall and thin, with hair to his shoulders and a long goatee. His hands were on his knees, fingers spread over them like spiders.

"I said, who the hell are you?" he said again.

"Sorry. I didn't know you were there. I mean, I didn't see you at first. I'm Ethan. I know Lydia from school."

"What do you want?"

"What? She invited me over."

"What do you want, though?"

"I don't know what you mean."

"What do you want from her? What are you going to do to her?"

I felt totally scared, like I was on trial and losing my case. "Nothing. I'm not going to do anything."

The guy narrowed his eyes and turned his gaze from the TV to me.

"Is that so? Is that a fact?"

There was a loud groaning sound of water fighting through bad pipes, a door opened down the hall, and Lydia came over.

"Leave him alone, Ryan. He's cool."

"Yeah, he seems real cool. Cool as a cucumber." He was still squinting at me.

"Come on," Lydia said. She grabbed my arm and pulled me away. "Ignore him. He's just like that."

"Um," I said. She pulled me to the stairs.

"See you, cool guy," he called.

Lydia took me up the stairs.

"Stay cool!" the guy from downstairs yelled.

There was a huge crack running up the wall next to the stairway. When we reached the second floor, there was a big hole in the wall, showing pipes and old wood framing. It occurred to me that I might end up being kept there as a prisoner, chained up in the house or something, like one of those stories you see on the eleven o'clock news. It would be the talk of the school: "Did you hear what happened to that Ethan kid? He went to that strange girl's house, and all they found were his bones and his backpack."

Lydia took me into her room. She closed the door behind her. The walls were freshly painted the same yellow you see in lemon pie, but the paint stopped about a foot short of the ceiling, like whoever had started got bored or moved on to some other project, or maybe just couldn't reach and didn't feel like getting a ladder or chair.

She pushed a button on her CD player and some sadcore song came on. A woman with a high voice who

sounded like she was heavily sedated whispered something about being wickedly split.

"I love this song," Lydia said.

"Who is this?"

"Ex Ex Woe. From Glasgow. You like it?"

"Sure. It's very cheerful."

"I'll burn you a copy. It grows on you."

"Cool. So who is that guy downstairs?" I asked.

"Ryan. That's my brother. Don't worry about him."

"What's his story?"

"Well, he kind of has issues. Just ignore him; you'll be
okay. But it'd be a good idea for you not to be alone with
him too much."

"Why not?"

She laughed. "Don't look that way. He won't hurt
you. Probably. I'm just saying. Don't be around him if I'm
not around. Sometimes he gets agitated."

"What do you mean by that?"

"Don't worry about it. Anyhow, we didn't come here
to talk about Ryan, did we?"

"I guess not."

She dropped down onto the bed. "Right. So let's do it."

I looked at her. She stared at me, totally open.
"What?" I said.

"Get to work. You have your script?"

"My script. Of course I have it." I dug in my backpack. My forehead was sweating, along with my back
and armpits. It was hot as hell in there.

We worked on the play for a while. The problem was that we didn't really have any scenes together. She worked on my scenes with me for a while. She was very good. She kept getting me to focus on the anger I was supposed to be feeling.

"Don't make anger," she said. "Look. If you were a big movie star and someone stole your part by selling a bunch of lies to the tabloids, how would you feel?"

"Mad."

"Mad? That's it? You know what? Don't put words to it. Feel the situation, stay in the moment, and the emotion will create itself."

"I'm trying to do what you're saying. It's hard."

"It is hard, but that's the way to do it. It'll come, you'll see."

We tried a little more, but I was getting confused. I didn't know how much to relax, how much to focus on what I was saying.

"You're getting all frustrated," she said.

"I don't know how much to concentrate on how I feel."

"Stop trying to analyze it. Don't work with your brain. Work with your heart."

Which was the opposite of what I'd been trying so hard to do for so long. It was different from what I was used to, but it sounded good.

"Let's try something different," she said. "We'll work on my scene. Forget that Duffy stuff. You're going to take the lead role for a while." She took my script and flipped through it. "Here, let's do this one."

It was a scene between Mike Beath and Lei-Dee, where they're plotting to kill the producer. Lydia went to the window and started talking. I read my lines. And it actually felt really good to be in this part.

"Stop concentrating so much on how you sound. You're acting too hard, you're practically mugging."

"I'm trying," I said. I didn't like how my voice sounded, too much like a little kid. I cleared my throat, making it as deep as I could.

"Look," she said. "These two are the only ones in the whole play who have a real, deep connection. They're passionately in love, they're alone in the world, and their bond is about to get a thousand times stronger, by the time they finish this moment together. They'll have taken a step they can't take back."

"No turning back. Got it."

"All right, then," she said. She took the script from me and tossed it on the bed.

"Wait. I don't know these lines," I said.

"That's okay. Because you know what this scene is about. That's enough. Just let it flow."

"Improvise."

"Yeah. Let's go," she said. She looked down at the floor for a couple of seconds, then turned back to me, her eyes blazing. "Now you listen to me," she said. "I'm not in the habit of hooking up with losers. You're going to get what's yours. Are you going to let some pretty-boy kid from Arkansas come into this town and bump you off the A-list?"

"I'm not off the A-list. I'm still . . . on top." I couldn't remember the exact lines.

"Yeah, well, when your agent is seen doing lunch with that kid, I'd say your days on top are numbered."

"What am I supposed to do about it?" I said. I didn't know exactly what the script said, but I had the right idea. "I mean, what, I can't *kill* the guy."

Her eyes narrowed, and her lips parted. She was good. I got a chill.

"People die in Hollywood all the time," she said. "Accidents, homicides. They happen every day."

"It can happen to anyone," I said quietly.

"It's hot in here," she said. I looked at her. She pulled the black sweater up over her head in one move. She tossed it on the floor. She was wearing a tiny Hello Kitty tank top.

"Yeah," I said. My voice was quieter than I thought it would be. I pulled off my flannel shirt, and stood there in my Hellboy T-shirt.

She put her hands on my chest. I wondered if she could feel my heart speed up.

I was stuck. It almost seemed like something else was going on, something besides rehearsing the scene. But thinking about that made me feel like a jerk, like the kind of guy Amanda had warned me against being. And it was better to ignore that whole feeling, because I knew that could get me into about ten kinds of trouble.

She looked down and then up again, into my eyes, looking for something, intense.

"You have the strength to take this step. It was what you were meant to do." She walked to the window and pointed at the sky. "It's in the stars. It's our fate."

"I know that. But it's dangerous." I took two steps closer and stood right behind her.

"Let your courage fill you. Let it make you big, strong. Be brave."

I didn't know what to say. I remembered that silence can be just as powerful as words, maybe more.

"We'll do this. Together," she said. "If you're brave enough. If you're man enough."

"I am."

Lydia leaned back, just a little, and her shoulder blades pressed into my chest. The curved backside of her black jeans just barely touched my hips.

I felt my breathing go unsteady. Were we still rehearsing? Lydia leaned back into me harder. She smelled like roses and cinnamon. This was something else.

She turned to me. She closed her eyes and tilted her head up. Her lips were just in front of mine. Her breath filled my mouth.

"Okay," she whispered. "That was good. That's enough."

And just like that, she was gone, across the room. Miles away.

❧ ❧

"Oh, here he is right now," Mom said when I walked in the door. She covered the mouthpiece and held the phone out to me like she was offering a gift. "It's Jane."

"Let me just get my coat off," I said. I was cold from the walk back from Lydia's house.

"And don't make it long. We're eating in a few minutes," Mom said.

I took the phone into the living room. "Hi," I said.

"Where were you?" Her tone was totally pissed off.

"What?"

"You heard me. Where were you?"

"What do you mean?"

"You're in honors English. I figure you can understand those words. Where. Were. You."

Act casual.

"I was rehearsing for the play."

"Oh, really? Where?"

"What is this?"

"I know where you were."

"What are you talking about?"

"I know you were with that girl. Lydia."

"What?" It was all I could come up with.

"So you call it 'rehearsing,' huh?"

"Listen." And just then, there was a call-waiting beep. Perfect timing.

"That's my other line."

"Don't you put me on hold."

"Hold on." I hit the flash button. "Hello?"

"Dude. It's Tim. Listen, dude." He always said *dude* when he was nervous. "I just wanted to give you a heads up. Jane is probably gonna call you. She's pissed."

"Too late. She's on the other line."

"Dude, I'm sorry. Maybe I messed up. She called me, totally worried, because she heard that your play practice was canceled. She couldn't find you, and she called me. I told her that I thought I saw you walking to the bike path with that girl Lydia Krane."

"You what? You told her that?"

"Dude, I'm sorry. Jane was freaking out. She was all worried. I was just trying to help."

"Oh, my God. Are you crazy? Thanks, Tim. That was great."

"Sorry. You and Jane aren't breaking up or anything, are you? That would totally suck."

"We're not breaking up. I don't think. I guess I'm about to find out."

"Because you're completely awesome together. Don't break up with her."

"I didn't want to, but thanks to you, now she probably wants to break up with me."

"Oh, dude. Don't say that. I mean I just said what I saw, which was the truth. I didn't tell you to go off with that girl. Dude, don't blame me."

"I gotta get back to Jane." I hit the flash button. There was nobody there. Jane had hung up. I speed dialed her number.

"That was real nice, leaving me on hold like that," she said.

"Listen, I was rehearsing before. I wouldn't lie to you. I'm going to be totally honest. Rehearsal was canceled, so Lydia Krane offered to help me."

"I'll bet."

"Nothing happened. Come on, you know I wouldn't do that."

"Do I? Know that?"

"I don't know, Jane. Do you?" I was able to take a surprisingly convincing self-righteous tone at being doubted.

"I don't like the idea of you going to her house, just you and her. It's not right. I don't like this. What's going on?"

"Nothing is going on. Look. You want me to come over?"

"Not really," she said. Her voice was low.

"I'm going to come over."

"Oh no you're not," Mom called from the kitchen. "You're not going anywhere. We're eating dinner in two minutes, and then you have to do your schoolwork."

"Mom, I have to see Jane."

"You 'have' to?" Jane said. "No thanks. I don't want to be an obligation to you."

"You'll see her tomorrow in school."

"I don't want to be some kind of burden."

"You have priorities. You wanted to be in the play, but you have to keep up with schoolwork. That was the deal."

"Don't bother coming over. I know you're real busy."

"Everyone is talking to me at once."

"'Bye," Jane said, and hung up.

"I don't know what's going on between you and Jane, but you'll have to figure it out tomorrow. You have too many things going on at once. I have nothing else to say about it," Mom said.

And finally, there was silence.

～ ～

Though I said to Tim that Jane might want to break up with me, I was mostly kidding. We'd been together for almost a year, and we'd known each other for a lot longer than that. I couldn't really imagine us breaking up. We were so used to hanging out together and talking on the phone all the time, I couldn't really imagine all that being gone. I had to assume she felt the same way. She'd been mad at me before, just like I'd gotten mad at her sometimes. It would blow over.

These were things I thought about as I sat by my window, looking out, that night.

But then there was the whole thing with Lydia Krane. I wasn't totally sure what she was thinking, but I had to admit: it was all kind of exciting. She was new, and she was unpredictable. Had I really done anything wrong?

Cloudy Boy. My X-ray portrait was curling at the edges. Some of the darker areas were getting lighter and fainter from being exposed all the time. Cloudy Boy was becoming transparent. So what about me?

I knocked lightly on Amanda's door. There was no answer. I knocked some more. Nothing.

I pushed her door open and put my face halfway in. It was cool in her room. She liked to keep her windows open partway.

"What?" she groaned.

"You're not nude or anything, are you?"

"No. I'm under the covers. What do you want?"

"Are you awake?"

"I am now."

"Good." I went in and sat on her little couch.

"Don't get all comfortable in here. I'm going to sleep."

"Okay. I just want your opinion on something."

"Oh, come on. I'm sleeping."

"Just one thing. Is there any way it can be called cheating if you haven't done anything at all?"

"You're cheating on Jane?" She suddenly sounded more awake.

"No. I'm just saying."

"What did you do?"

"Nothing."

"If it's nothing, then why are you asking?"

I looked past her curtains to the silhouette of the tree Dad had planted about nine years ago. It had been as short as me when we put it in, and now it grew higher than her window. All the leaves were gone now. It looked skinny, stripped naked.

"Let's say the guy hangs out with another girl."

"Who?"

"Come on. Can't you just answer?"

"First tell me who she is."

"Fine. You don't know her. She's another sophomore. Lydia Krane is her name."

"Don't know her."

"I told you. So if I just hang around with her, it's not cheating, right? There's no way you could call it cheating. Right?"

"Depends."

"On what?"

"On how you feel about her."

Oh, crap. "What do you mean?"

"You know what I mean. If you *like* her like her and you're hanging out with her?"

"I'm taking the fifth."

"Uh-huh. Well, you know how you feel."

"Okay. But you haven't answered my question. It's not cheating if nothing happened. Right?"

"Here's one way to test it. Ask yourself this: Am I doing anything that I wouldn't want Jane to know about?"

"Not really." Well, yeah.

"If that's true, then I guess you're probably okay."

"Good. Okay. Maybe you should go to sleep. It's pretty late."

"Thanks. Now I'm all awake."

"Count sheep," I said. I got up and went to the door.

"And by the way," Amanda said.

"What?"

"If you're not a better liar with Jane than you are with me, then you're in big, big trouble."

RANDOM JABS

I got up early and went to school at six. It was still dark, and I could barely see the fog on the pond as I passed. I got into the pool area through the side door on the second floor and sat up in the bleachers.

The air was warm, humid, with that chlorine smell. Every sound and whistle and yell bounced off the tiled walls. Jane was totally at home in the indoor pool area. I felt like I was in a suffocating sweat box. Nobody was supposed to watch girls' swim practice since a custodian found some perverted notes up on the bleachers last year.

I needed to patch things up with Jane. I watched her swim. She was so strong. I wished I could swim like that. She always downplayed her strengths. Like how she was really pretty smart, but didn't believe it. She was probably smarter than I was.

The sudden shrill sound of coach's whistle blasted off the tile walls and shot into my eardrums like ice picks. I cringed and put my hands over my ears. The girls got out of the water and wrapped towels around themselves. I walked down the bleachers and toward the locker room, where all the girls were heading.

"Hey," Ms. Sweeney, the coach, said. "You don't belong in here."

"I have to give a message to Jane Landau. It's important."

"You can't come in here. You'll have to see her later." Just then, Jane came up to find out what was going on.

"Your mom said that you need to walk your brother to the doctor after school for his allergy shots," I said.

"Today?" Jane said.

"Yeah. She said he'll swell up like a balloon if you don't take him."

"Okay," the coach said. "Talk to her, but next time you'll have to wait until she comes out of the locker room."

The coach followed the last of the girls into the locker room. Jane stood there, looking past my shoulder. "So which of my brothers is so allergic?"

"Uh, that would be Iggy."

"Really. Not Lorenzo?"

"Lorenzo's fine."

"Well, that's a relief. It's also nice to learn that I have brothers."

"Best I could come up with on the spot."

Jane pretended to be interested in a tile on the floor. She was starting to shiver.

"Look," I said. "About yesterday. I'm telling you, we were rehearsing for the play. That's all."

Jane shrugged.

"You believe me, right?"

"Should I?"

"Yes. Don't you know I'm an honest guy? Ask anybody." I gave her a big grin, trying to make her smile. She turned away.

"Are you smiling at me, or still mad?"

"I'm still mad, but not as much. I don't like you going to her house. It's not right."

"Okay."

She turned back to me. She squeezed her hair out, and it splashed on the floor. "So that's done, right?" she said. "You won't go to her house again."

"I don't see why I would. I don't even really have any scenes with her, you know."

"All right. Let's just, I don't know. Get past this."

"Good. So I'll let you go change. First bell is going to be pretty soon."

"There's a party at Steve Piccini's house tonight. Let's go."

"We don't know him."

"Nora's cousin is going out with his sister's boyfriend."

"I didn't understand that."

"You don't have to. It means we can go."

"It's a date."

≈ ≈

"Is it true you guys are breaking up?" Scott said to me in the hallway.

"What are you talking about?"

"Nora said she talked to Tim, and he said there's something going on. That you and Jane had this mega-fight and that you fooled around with some girl and all this stuff."

"I'm gonna kill Tim."

"I never said that," Tim said after second period. "That's totally not what I said. You better talk to Nora."

So I talked to Nora, who also denied it. I hated this kind of stuff. I waited until we got to lunch.

"We're still together. There's no problem. Everything's perfect," I announced to the table.

"Of course," Nora said. "Who would say different?"

"Sounds like all of you would," Jane said.

"And I thought you had mono, Itsy," I said.

"Faking. Didn't want to take the English test. I'm all recovered."

"Good one," Tim said.

"Not really. You need to pick something more credible than getting mono," I said.

"Shut up. There are other ways to get mono, you know," Nora said.

"Yeah," Jane agreed. "And besides. She *could* have a boyfriend."

"Could, but doesn't," Scott said.

"Disgusting," Tim said, examining his sandwich.

It seemed like everything was back to normal.

I told them I was getting some ice cream or something. When I got to the front, I was surprised to bump into Lydia.

"What are you doing here? You never come to this period lunch," I said.

"Just wanted a drink," she said. She held up a can of soda. "Where are you sitting?"

I felt stuck. I knew it would be totally uncomfortable and awkward if I brought her to the table to sit with Jane and the others. I worried that Jane might be nasty to Lydia, or Lydia might be mean to Jane, and I absolutely didn't want to get caught in the middle.

"Well, I'm not really sitting anywhere. I'm just around," I said.

"What are you talking about? I know you're sitting with your wife and those friends of yours. Don't look so worried. I'm not going to come over."

"Okay. But I mean you could. If you want. Of course you could."

"Thanks, but no thanks. I'm heading back to the library."

"All right. I'll see you later?"

She leaned in close and whispered. "That was great yesterday. I feel close to you."

To my total shock, she tucked her fingers in the back pocket of my jeans. It was quick, and my back was to the wall, so nobody could have seen it.

She went off in the direction of the library. I waited a minute and then headed back to the table. Act casual, act casual.

"I thought you were getting some ice cream or something." Nora said. "You don't have anything."

"Oh. I just changed my mind. There wasn't anything I wanted."

Tim went back to pulling the lid off a tiny can of cling peaches. His eating habits were strictly second grade.

"So why didn't you bring her back to the table?" Jane asked.

"Who?" I said, trying to sound casual.

Jane glared at me.

"Who, Lydia? Yeah. I said hello. But she's not—"

If looks could kill, I'd have been six feet under.

Five minutes before, I'd thought everything was fine. Now I was back in big trouble.

❧ ❧

"When I call your name, come up and I will show you your grade for the marking period," Mr. Dugan said. "In the meantime, solve the problems on pages eighty-five and eighty-six. I'll be collecting your work at the end of the period."

As he called out names and kids went to peer into the grade book, I tried to figure out what my average was. Even with that A he ended up giving me for the objective test, by my calculations, I was looking at an eighty-two.

Mom and Dad wouldn't be too thrilled. It was going to take some doing to convince them to let me stay in the play.

"Ethan Lederer," he called. I went up. He didn't look at me. He pointed with a rigid finger at a small box in his grade book. Inside the box was written 95. Wrong box.

"Where?" I said.

He tapped hard with his finger at the box, then pointed at it with the tip of his pen.

"What?" I said. "That can't be right."

"What's the matter, you think it's unfair? Not high enough?"

"No. It's not that."

"Take your seat. Michael Millet."

I went back to my seat. I felt crappy.

When the bell rang, I waited for all the kids to leave, and then I went to Mr. Dugan at his desk.

"Hi. I wanted to talk to you about this grade."

He snapped his grade book shut and walked past me and into the hallway. Weird. I followed him.

"Mr. Dugan?"

"You think I'm going to be alone in a classroom with you? So you can accuse me of something else I didn't do?"

Wow. His voice sounded all different, choked, without the strict tone he usually had. The guy was scared. That wasn't at all what I'd wanted.

"I know I don't deserve a ninety-five."

"Is this another trick? Is there something else you want to threaten me with?"

"No. It's not like that."

He looked around to make sure there were plenty of kids in the hallway. He got a little closer to me and leaned in. He spoke just loud enough for me to hear him.

"You listen to me. I went to MIT. I won awards. And I have worked in this school for eleven years. I'm good at what I do. I'm smart, some might say gifted. You, on the other hand, are not. You're a poser; you're a pretender. You do not belong in this honors class. You certainly don't deserve any kind of passing grade. But you and your little girlfriend have put me in a bad position with your lies and innuendo. Blackmail, fine. So you'll get your A, you'll get them all year, and I won't say anything. But don't come to me with questions, and don't talk to me, don't even look at me, because our business is done."

His face was that bright red color again.

"And one other thing, don't you dare come to me with this innocent act. Because I'm on to you. I know exactly what you really are. You know, and I know. And one day, I can assure you, you're going to pay for this."

"Are you threatening me?"

"I would never threaten you," he said in mocking voice. "I'm just stating a fact. Someday, somehow, you are going to pay."

He turned, went into the lab, and slammed the door.

I looked to see if anyone else in the hall had heard. Nobody was looking; everyone was just going their own way, talking, shouting, moving to get somewhere else.

Nobody knew what was happening with me. None of them knew anything.

❧ ❦

"When I went to him, I kind of felt bad, but the way he acted got me all pissed off. Calling me a pretender? Saying I'm not smart? What kind of a teacher is that?" I said to Lydia.

"I'd say a pretty crappy one," she said in the Southern accent. We were in a corner of the library. I knew that Nora and Tim were in class, so there was no chance either of them would see us and cause me more trouble with Jane. "And this just shows you that you have nothing at all to feel bad about. The guy is a total scumbag. This is justice."

"What do you think he meant when he said I would pay?"

"Nothing. He's just mad and wants to scare you. He can't do anything. Even if I can't prove that he touched me, the accusation and the investigation would ruin him, and he knows it. He can't do anything to us."

"I don't know."

"That's okay, because I do. Don't worry."

She smiled at me. I smiled back.

I was worried.

❧ ❦

Rehearsal felt better. I thought I was doing a better job of what Lydia taught me: not creating emotion, but letting the feelings happen. I surprised myself a few times when my voice came out bolder or more vicious than I had planned. I guessed that was what it felt to really get into the character. When we finished, I was putting my script into my backpack, and Jordan Paul came over to me and said, "That was some rehearsal, huh?"

"Yeah, I guess so."

"I had a couple of ideas about your part. Interested?"

"Sure."

He nodded his head toward the lighting cage behind the heavy curtains. I followed him. I wasn't sure if I needed notes from him, considering he was stumbling over a lot of his own lines and seemed to be having a hard time understanding what was going on in the play. Still, this was the first time he had ever made any move to be friendly, much less even notice me.

We got to the cage, and he leaned against it like James Dean. It was pretty dark, and half his face was in shadow. Still, I could see when he smiled at me. It made me wish I looked like him.

"So here's the thing," he said. "I'm not sure you understand something."

"What's that?"

"Well, I don't think you understand who has the lead role in this play."

"I don't know what you mean."

"All that big acting you're doing. Well, that's all fine, but not when I'm in the lead. Don't go trying to steal my lightning."

"Thunder."

"What?" he said.

"It's thunder that gets stolen, not lightning."

"Well, whatever. Phil is too nice a guy to say anything. But I'm telling you now to back off. You're a supporting player, and that's it. Don't you go trying to grab the spotlight or you'll be sorry. Capisce?"

"Yeah," I said. "Capisce." Why was everybody threatening me today?

"Good," he said. He threw the curtains open in what I'm sure he thought was a dramatic exit. It left a lot of dust swirling in the red and blue lights.

"What was that all about with the master thespian?" Lydia asked me on the way past the pond.

"Oh, nothing. He wanted to talk to me about my performance."

"Who, that moron? He's a terrible actor. How is he going to give you notes?"

"Well, to tell you the truth, I think he's feeling a little like I'm upstaging him or something."

"You are. Because you're good and he's bad. That's not your problem."

"It is if he doesn't like it."

"Did he threaten you?" She stopped walking and grabbed my jacket sleeve. There was something about the look in her eyes that made me a little nervous.

"He didn't threaten me."

"Listen, that idiot shouldn't even be on the stage,

unless he's sweeping it after the show. You should be the lead. He has a lot of nerve coming to you like that."

"Don't say anything to him, all right?"

"Why?"

"I'm just saying. Don't. Promise you won't say anything to him."

"I won't say anything to him, I promise. Okay?"

"Thank you. Anyway." We started walking again.

"Anyway. You feel like coming over?"

"Oh. Well, I can't. I kind of have some plans."

"Really? Big Friday night?"

"Nothing big."

"I understand."

We walked quietly for a while. Over the tops of the bare trees, I could see the power lines stretching far and then curving around a bend in the bike trail, disappearing out of view. Lydia kicked a rock into the pond. She seemed a little sad.

"Are you doing anything tonight?" I said. As I said the words, I worried that I was opening up something that could be trouble.

"Me? Yeah. I have big plans."

"You sure?"

"Yep."

"Because there's a party, I think." I didn't know why I said it. I couldn't have invited her. Not without Jane hiring someone to kill me.

"Are you going?"

"Yeah."

"With your wife?"

"Um. Yeah."

"Well, have fun. I have my own plans."

I knew she didn't have plans, but I was relieved that she didn't want to come to the party.

❧ ❧

The party was turning out to be no fun at all. I'd had hopes that it was going to get Jane and me back to where we used to be, but it didn't look like that was going to happen. Not with me on one side of the room with a bunch of guys, watching a huge plasma TV that was showing a Pay-Per-View boxing match I had no interest in, and Jane just barely visible through the kitchen door, talking to Nora and some girl I didn't know, probably about what a jerk I was.

I should have known this was going to be a bad night starting from the car ride over. Amanda drove us to the party. Of course, Amanda and Jane really liked each other. They talked about a girl on the swim team they both knew. It was like I wasn't even in the car at all, so I didn't pay much attention to their conversation. I was thinking about the homework I had to catch up on. I had to work on outlining a paper about point of view in *The Great Gatsby*, and I was going to have to start research for a history paper on the economic state of Germany between the wars. As long as Lydia wasn't planning on blackmailing all of my teachers, I still had to keep the grades up. Going to this party was going to lose me a few hours of time for homework, which meant that I'd have to make it up on the weekend.

"This is it, right?" Amanda said, slowing to a stop.

"This is it. Thanks so much for the ride," Jane said.

"How are you getting home?" Amanda asked.

"We can try to get a ride with someone," I said.

"I'm not coming out again after eleven. If it's before then, you can call."

"Thanks," Jane said. "You're the best."

"Any time," Amanda said.

It was kind of a strange group at the party, with a lot of kids we didn't know. There were some kids from Jane's classes, but none from mine. A lot of kids from other towns. Tim, Scott, and Nora were already there and practically knocked us over when they saw us.

We hung around the living room for a while. The music was good, and the throbbing bass gave me a cool vibrating feeling in the back of my skull. It was also totally packed with people, shouting, hooting, laughing, dancing. I don't dance, which Jane knew, so she didn't even bother asking. She would dance with Nora, if she wanted to.

We wandered around as a little pack for a while, trying to see if there was anybody interesting we knew. Some kid from Jane's math class called out, "Hey. What are *you* doing here?" What a great question. We came to see if we could develop a plan for world peace.

After a while, we settled in the kitchen. Some kid in a varsity baseball jacket from another town was standing there with two girls. He had an open bag of chocolate chips. In front of him was a small yappy dog, who sat up on its back legs and then when it started paddling the air with its front paws, the baseball player said, "Good spastic dog," and tossed a chocolate chip for the dog to snap out of the air.

"Isn't chocolate really bad for dogs?" Jane asked me.

"Yeah. I think it makes them break out."

"No, I'm serious. I thought it could kill them or something."

"I don't know about that. I think it's a myth."

"It's true," Scott said. "I read it."

"Where?" I said.

"In a magazine, I think."

I laughed. "Which magazine would you read that would have that information? *Dangerous Canine Snackies Monthly?*"

"Why do you think you always know everything?" Jane said to me in a sharp tone. "Are you the expert on every single subject?"

I looked at her. "We're just kidding around."

"It's okay," Scott said.

"No, it pisses me off. You can't feed chocolate to dogs; it'll kill them. So just because you think you know everything, this dog could end up dead. Is that what you want?"

"Jane?"

She was all pissed off. "You know everything. But maybe, just maybe, you're wrong. And the dog dies for it."

"I think you're taking this a little too seriously. But fine." I turned to the baseball player. "Hey, you know? Aren't dogs allergic to chocolate?"

"Not this one. He loves it," the baseball player said. He crumpled up the bag. "But we're all out anyways. Hey. Let's see if he likes scotch. Come on, doggie." The baseball player and the girls left the kitchen, with the dog following at their heels.

"I wouldn't do that," I called to them. "I think that dog is in rehab. He's on, like, step ten," I called. Scott and Tim broke up. I turned to Jane. "Happy?" I said.

"Oh, yeah. I'm thrilled. That was so funny."

I shook my head and wandered out of the kitchen. Scott and Tim followed.

"What was that about?" I asked.

"I don't know," Tim said. "I was gonna ask you. She seems like she's in a real bad mood."

"I'll say," Scott said. "What's going on over there?" What was going on was a keg. We each got a plastic cup of beer. I didn't get one for Jane, since she wouldn't drink at all. I wasn't much of a drinker either, but I just felt like it then, kind of tense.

We went through the living room and saw a bunch of guys sitting on the couch, on chairs, and standing around the huge TV while two boxers got instructions from a referee. That was the end of Scott. He found a spot behind the couch, I could just barely hear him say to the guy next to him, "Boxing is a sport, but it's not real fighting." Scott's eyes were fixed on the screen. We wouldn't be seeing Scott for a while.

Tim and I went back into the kitchen. Jane looked at the half cup of beer in my hand.

"I'm having one cup of beer, if that's okay," I said.

"Are you going to get all drunk and make an ass of yourself singing with a bunch of guys on the dining room table?"

"Oh, my God. That happened one time. One time! Are you ever going to let that go?"

"You guys broke the table. It was so embarrassing, I couldn't believe it. It was like you were some other person who I didn't even know. Or want to know. Is that on your sched for tonight?"

I shook my head and turned away again, went right back into the living room. I wondered what Lydia was doing at that moment. On the TV, the boxers took random jabs at each other, testing, testing. Everyone in the living room shouted directions at them, like that was going to help. They were a thousand miles away from us and couldn't hear any advice from the people in this room. They probably couldn't even hear advice from the people at ringside. They were in their fight alone.

WEIRD THINGS

There was major tension at the lunch table. Or at least I felt it, anyway. Jane and I didn't really talk directly to each other much. It was pretty much the Tim Food Show for most of the period.

When the five-minute bell rang, we cleared our stuff and launched it at the garbage can from ten feet away, standing clear of the strike zone.

As we were walking toward the double doors, I knew I was supposed to ask The Question. Knowing the answer, or not knowing it, didn't matter. You have to ask. It's one of the Avoid the Doghouse rules.

"Everything okay?" I said to Jane.

"Sure," she said. Expected. Then, "Why?"

"I don't know. You seem quiet or something."

"Not really," she said. Then she waited. I figured she was working from a rule in the girl's playbook, something like "make him work for it." Either that, or she was really pissed.

"Well, it seems like something."

"You mean besides not seeing me or calling all week-end? Besides that?"

"I told you after the party on Friday. I said I had to work all weekend to catch up on stuff. I told you that."

"Yeah. And so you didn't even have five minutes to call? Especially after how things went at the party?"

She stopped walking and looked at me. Okay, she was pissed. I was at least halfway in the doghouse, and I had no idea how to wiggle out. I stood there with my hands out and facing up, like in a helpless pose, my mouth half open. I tried to come up with a good answer, and I came up totally blank.

"Right," she said. "That's great." She started walking again. A flapping noise passed over me. Someone sailed a textbook like a Frisbee. A tall kid got hit in the back of the head, and he screamed out a bunch of curses. Most of the kids laughed.

I trotted after Jane. Since rehearsal that afternoon was going to be scenes that I wasn't in, I was excused. So maybe I could score some good-guy points.

"You want to come over after school?" I said.

"Don't you have play practice?"

"Not today. Why don't you come over."

"To do what?"

To do what? When did we ever need a planned activity? What was happening? "Just to hang."

"You want me to?"

"Of course." It was the only answer, even if I wasn't totally sure it was true.

She took a minute to think about it. "Okay," she said. "Sounds good. I'll wait for you at the place."

∽ ∾

"I have a lot of books I need to use," Jane said. "I don't know if I can do it lying down."

"Me, too," I said. So we ended up working at the kitchen table, instead of our usual place on the couch, or in my room. I really wanted to say something, anything to break the silence, but I didn't know what, so I just kept my mouth shut.

"Could you please stop tapping?" Jane said.

"What?"

"That tapping with your pen. It's very distracting. Could you stop?"

"Sorry."

I put my pen down and turned a page, and I worried that I'd turned it too loudly. Then I wondered if I was breathing too loudly, too. This was crazy. I'd never, ever felt uncomfortable with Jane, and now I felt like I had to worry if my breathing was too loud.

"What's going on?" I said.

"What?"

"I'm saying. What is going on? Why is this happening?"

Jane looked at me. "I'm just sitting here. What's the problem?"

Fine. If she didn't want to talk about it, then that was just fine. I turned back to my history book. I read for a while, but it didn't make sense. I realized I was reading the same two sentences about Germany's war debt over and over. Then I heard Jane breathing, and her breath caught. I looked up.

She was gazing down at her book, and I saw a big fat tear drop from the end of her nose to the page. Then another one.

"Jane?"

"How can you ask me what's going on?"

The phone rang. I stared at her. It rang again.

"Well, answer it," she said. She wiped roughly at her eyes. I looked down at the table. Jane always hated to cry. "Go answer it."

I got up and answered the phone. "Hello?"

"You missed a very interesting rehearsal today," Lydia said.

"Oh, yeah?" I watched Jane, trying not to let on who was on the phone.

"Very, very interesting."

"Well, that's great. I'd love to hear about it, but now's not a good time."

"Why not?"

"Mom should be home in about an hour or so," I said into the phone.

"What?" Lydia said.

"You want me to have her call you?"

"Oh, I get it. Your wife is there. Yes, definitely have your mom call me."

"She has your number."

"I'm so bored. Let's talk for a really, really long time. How's that sound?"

"Well, I can't say for sure. So I'll have her call you."

"Hey, I know. Have you ever had phone sex?"

"Uh, sure, that's fine. Is there anything else?"

She laughed. "Is this a convenient time to try it? You start."

"Okay, I have to go now."

"Fine. I'll start. What are you wearing?"

I hung up the phone and went back to the table.

"Who was that?" Jane asked.

"That? That was my cousin."

"Which one?"

"That was Emily. You met her, right?"

"Yes, I met Emily." Jane pursed her lips, pushed the chair back from the table, and started putting her books in her bag.

"What are you doing?" I asked her.

She breathed in sharply through her nose and cleared her throat. "You remember that time last summer when we went to the mall and you snuck off with Scott for a while? And I asked you where you went and you said you went to Sports Authority to look at sneakers. I asked you again, and you said, 'I told you. Sneakers.' And then that night you gave me those onyx earrings that I'd been looking at."

I nodded, confused. She smiled, and when she breathed in, I heard her voice catch again. She swallowed, overcoming the urge to cry. "Well, I learned two things about you that day. One was that you can be really sweet and thoughtful." She took a breath and calmed herself again. "The other thing? You may be a good actor, but you're a terrible liar."

Jane pulled on her jacket.

"I know you too well. I learned that day about the tiny twitch you get in the corner of your eye when you lie. I first saw it that day, when you talked about the sneakers. I've seen it a few times since then. Every time I saw it, I always knew you were lying."

She slung her backpack over her shoulder.

"And I saw it now. That wasn't your cousin Emily. That was *her*." She pulled the door open and stepped outside. "And you have the nerve to ask me what's going on? *That's* what's going on."

"Jane. Come on. I didn't . . ." I trailed off. There wasn't much to say. I couldn't look her in the eye. She turned away from me. I stood on the front step and watched as she walked down the front path to the street.

"Can I walk with you?" I said.

"No."

"Jane. I'm sorry I didn't tell you it was her. But I knew it would bother you."

"You were right."

"Are we breaking up?" I called.

"See that? See how smart you are?"

I went out to the street. The cold from the asphalt went right through my socks and into the soles of my feet.

"You should know. There's nothing happening between me and her. Nothing."

"You just keep on saying that, Ethan. Maybe you'll start to believe it."

I thought of calling out to her, but I had nothing to say. I pictured running after her, but it felt fake. So I stood there in the middle of the street until she passed over the rise and disappeared from sight.

❧ ❧

I kept waking up all night, rolling over and over, as if changing my position would help. It felt like there was an insane DJ in my head, playing these endless samples of songs that I couldn't shake, plus repeating things Jane and Lydia had said, over and over.

So I wasn't exactly at my sharpest when I got to school. I was about to go upstairs to English when a hand grabbed my arm and pulled me under the stairway. Who else could it be: Lydia.

"So don't you want to know what I called you about?" She was Southern today.

"Sure. What?"

"What's the matter with you?"

"Nothing. Why?"

"Sounding a little snappy there."

"I'm just tired."

"Oh, wait. I didn't get you in trouble with the missus when I called yesterday, I hope. I mean, I kind of figured you were allowed to get phone calls."

"It's nothing. What did you want to tell me about rehearsal?" Footsteps pounded on the stairway above our heads.

"Oh. Well, it's pretty funny."

"What."

"And thrilling, actually."

"What?"

"But you'll see later."

"Can you please just tell me what it is?"

"Nope. You shouldn't have hung up on me last night. Now you'll have to wait."

She walked out from under the stairway, and I followed.

"Did something happen?" I asked her. She came back to me, put her hand on the back of my neck. It sent sort of a shiver through me. She pulled my head close to hers, and we were cheek to cheek. "You'll see soon enough," she whispered. Her breath buzzed inside my ear. "It's really good."

She let me go and walked away. I looked after her.

Of course, who was standing there but Jane, with Nora and Scott behind her.

"Nice twitch," Jane said.

"What?"

She touched the corner of her eye, gave me the finger,

and walked away from me. Nora and Scott followed her.

And all before eight in the morning.

∽ ∾

I didn't exactly hurry to get to lunch. I milled around outside the caf until about ten minutes into the period. I went in just far enough to see the table where we usually sat. The usual suspects were there, except for me, of course. Jane was talking, looking at the top of the table, and the others were all listening to her. Nora had one hand on Jane's shoulder and was leaning in close. No way was I going to be able to go there. And I wasn't about to go sit at some other table with kids I hardly knew, or barely liked.

So it looked like I'd be spending my lunch periods in the library.

∽ ∾

I got back a ninety-two on a math test, and a ninety-four on a history paper. My schoolwork was looking pretty solid. Major relief.

There had been a notice on the auditorium doors that the full cast needed to show up for a short meeting.

When I got to the auditorium, everyone was already gathered up front by the stage. Lydia was there. Jordan Paul was at the piano, slowly picking out notes with one finger. Two of the DramaRamas were leaning on the piano like groupies in a lounge. The rest of the kids were milling around or looking at their scripts. I dropped my bag on a seat in the second row. Lydia was sitting on the edge of the stage.

"What's this about?" I asked her.

"We'll see in a moment, won't we?" She was British today.

"Why do I have the feeling that you know something I don't know?"

She shrugged.

Mr. Lombardi came in and placed his books on the long table in front of the stage. "Afternoon, gang. We'll start in a few minutes. Ethan, a word?" He waved me over to the five stairs at the side of the stage. I followed him up and into the wing, behind the heavy green curtain.

"You've been doing a wonderful job with your role. You have much better technique this year than you've had before."

"Wow. Thanks." I looked down. I felt really proud. And he thought it was worth pulling me aside to tell me.

"I wanted to tell you before telling the rest of the cast. Jordan Paul and I had a long conversation. The demands of the play, of the rehearsal schedule, are more than he can manage right now."

"How could that be? He lives for the plays. What would be more important to him?"

"I couldn't say. But the fact of the matter is that he's stepping aside. And you'll be taking the role."

I actually couldn't understand what he meant. "What do you mean, taking the role?"

"I'm asking you to take over the role of Mike Beath." The lead. Was he telling me I got the lead?

"Wait. You mean you want me to do the part during rehearsals for a while?"

"No. I'm saying you'll play the part."

It didn't make any sense. He was actually giving me the part. I would be playing the lead role in the play.

"There's nothing to be scared about," he said.

"Scared?"

"You look a little scared."

"No. I just don't get it. I'm kind of shocked."

"You do want the part, though."

"Sure I want the part."

"I have total confidence in you. Sorry to spring it on you like this. I could have called you out of class today. But frankly, I can't resist the drama. Let's go tell everybody."

My feet felt tingly as I followed him back out to the auditorium. As soon as we came out, I saw Lydia smiling at me. She knew.

"Well. Are we all here?" he said. "I won't keep you long, but we have some important things to talk about. We're going to have a cast change. Jordan Paul has some other commitments that are conflicting with the heavy rehearsal schedule, since the character of Mike Beath is in nearly every scene. I'm pleased to say that we won't be losing Jordan Paul from the production, but he will take a part that has a less exhaustive time requirement. So Jordan Paul will take the role of Mark Duffy.

And our current Duffy, Ethan Lederer, will take the role of Mike Beath."

Everyone turned and looked at me. My face froze. I didn't know whether to try to smile or if that would make me seem conceited or arrogant or something. I probably ended up looking like a deer caught in the headlights.

Mr. Lombardi grinned at me. "And I'm sure you all share my confidence that he will do an amazing job with the part."

I looked over at Jordan Paul. He looked less than thrilled.

"Since we have this significant change, we're going to put off rehearsal today so that our recast actors can have a chance to look at their parts before we dig in. So we'll see you all tomorrow."

Everybody gathered their stuff and headed up the aisles to the back of the auditorium. I watched Jordan Paul pull on his jacket. I felt like I should say something to him, but I couldn't imagine what. Thanks? Too bad? You'll be awesome in the other role? There wasn't anything I could think of that wouldn't sound like I was trying to rub it in or something. I watched him stalk over to one of the exit doors and push his way out, letting in a blast of sunlight.

Mr. Lombardi came over to me and patted me on the shoulder. "Congratulations."

"This is weird."

"Well, try and get over that. Make this role your own. The show, as they say, must go on."

❧ ❧

Lydia was waiting outside the auditorium for me. She held up her hand for a high five. I looked at her.

"What did you do?"

"What? I didn't do anything."

"Why in the world would Jordan Paul give up the lead in the play? Answer: Not by choice."

I opened the door and held it for Lydia, then followed her out. We headed for the path to the woods.

"What are you saying?"

I shook my head. "I'm saying that I know that guy, and he didn't give up that part because he was too busy with other things. Someone convinced him that he had to give it up, or forced him to do it. And I have this feeling that that someone just might be you."

"I didn't say a word to him."

"Really?"

"Really."

We walked awhile in silence. When we got to the pond, Lydia started talking again. "To tell you the truth, I think Mr. Lombardi figured out that Jordan and I just didn't have any chemistry. And on top of that, it was getting to be so obvious that Jordan Paul didn't even understand the play. My guess is that Mr. Lombardi wanted someone with some talent and brains in the lead role. And he also probably could sense the fireworks we might make playing opposite each other."

"And you had nothing to do with it?"

"Why do you keep asking me that?"

"Because this whole thing seems pretty weird to me."

"You know, it always amazes me when people say they can't believe something happened because it's weird, or unexpected, or whatever. I mean, what *isn't* weird?"

"It seems like, lately, more weird and unexpected stuff happens in life than so-called normal things."

"Right," she said. "Exactly. What's weird is normal, and what's normal is weird."

I shook my head. "Sometimes it's like my whole life is weird."

"Tell me about it."

Lydia stopped walking and grabbed me. She turned me to face her. She took my hands.

"But that's what I'm telling you," she said. "There's nothing weird about this. This is the way it was meant to be. This is all what was supposed to happen."

And when those eyes looked into mine, she made my worries and fears about her melt away. She was unusual. She was exciting.

Something became clear to me then. Jane and I broke up for a reason. It was so I could accept the truth.

I was in love with Lydia.

MAKING WAVES

Everyone in English was reading the brief bio of F. Scott Fitzgerald that was in our copies of *The Great Gatsby*. Everyone except Lydia, who was writing in her green journal, and me, who was watching Lydia.

"Okay, folks," Ms. Wagner said. "You can read the rest of the bio for homework. I'm really excited to get started with the book. It's one of my all-time favorites."

I was not excited to get started with the book. I had tried reading it on my own, but I stopped about a quarter of the way through, totally bored. I didn't get why everyone loved it so much. But on the other hand, it was a classic or whatever, so obviously the gazillion people who liked it were right and I was wrong.

"This book has everything. It has shattered dreams, love, mystery, violence, and murder." She was on a roll. "It looks at the death of the American Dream, at how a man creates a fantasy version of himself to get back a lost love and recapture the past."

She looked at us for a reaction. Just about everyone

seemed really interested. I tried to make sure I looked as interested as they did.

Ms. Wagner looked at Lydia. "Did you have something to say, Lydia? You look unhappy."

"Not unhappy. Just not impressed."

"With what?"

"With this book. With him."

Ms. Wagner kept the pleasant smile on her face, but I knew she wasn't too thrilled. "Have you read it?" she said.

"Yes. And I think it's a lot of crap."

That got the attention of pretty much everyone in the class. Ms. Wagner nodded. I got nervous that Lydia was about to go too far.

"Really? Okay," Ms. Wagner said slowly. "So, if you want to call an icon of American literature a lot of crap, I'm sure you have some specifics to back up your evaluation."

"Well, look at what Fitzgerald was like. Total bastard. He locked up his sick wife in a nuthouse, and once she was out of the way, he went out and lived it up."

"Okay, that may be, but what does that have to do with the book itself?"

"Because he makes it out like he's criticizing the corrupt morals of the people in the book when he was no better than that himself. It's totally hypocritical."

"Even if I agreed with you that he was a hypocrite and

dishonest about his belief in what he's writing, it doesn't mean the *book* is bad, does it?"

"It does to me. It's like, put up or shut up."

Ms. Wagner kept the smile on her face, but her lips got thin, and it was clear she was tense.

After class, I met Lydia in the hallway. "I think you made Ms. Wagner upset."

"Sorry. She asked what I thought and I told her."

"She loves that book."

"She can love it all she wants. I don't."

"I didn't like it too much either."

"Then why didn't you say something? Why don't you ever speak your mind?"

"I do. Sometimes."

She gave me a look. "Who does this sound like? 'Hey, I'll just keep my mouth shut and be the good boy. Don't make waves.' Sound like anyone you know?"

"Well, why should I make waves?"

"Because you know what doesn't have waves? A swamp." She stopped walking and pushed open the door to the girls' bathroom. Just before she slipped in, she said, "You want to be in a swamp or on the high seas?"

Good question. But it seemed to me you could drown in either one.

❧ ❧

I got a little jittery outside the auditorium just before rehearsal. I'd never had the lead in a play before.

The auditorium door opened, and Lydia came out.

"There you are. Everyone's inside, waiting for you. Why are you just standing there?"

"I'm coming. Just getting ready."

She tilted her head at me in that way of hers. "Nervous?"

"Yeah, a little."

"It's just another rehearsal."

"Yeah, with me suddenly in the lead."

"You don't want the part?"

"I know what you're doing. Yes, I want the part. But I can still be nervous."

"Okay, so be nervous." She yanked the door open.

Actually, I was surprised at how good it felt to do the part. I could use my nervous feeling, because Mike Beath was nervous. The whole idea of taking something on and having to question whether I was the right guy for the job was exactly what was happening to my character.

There was only one thing about the rehearsal that bothered me, and that was the way Jordan Paul kept kind of glaring at me over the top of his script. At first I thought maybe he was doing it to try to make me nervous so I'd screw up and everyone would think it was a big mistake for me to take over for him.

"That was a great rehearsal," Mr. Lombardi said when we finished. "I'm really happy with the way this is going. Thank you. See you all tomorrow." He caught my eye and nodded, like *good job*. Knowing that he was happy made me much more relaxed.

"I told you," Lydia said when we got out of rehearsal. "And you were worried."

"It felt okay. It was fun."

"Come on over for dinner," she said.

"Oh, thanks, but I have a lot of homework."

"You could do it with me."

"What?"

"Your homework. You could do it with me, if you want. We'll eat, do homework; we can even rehearse some."

I looked at her. She gave me that smile.

"I'm not coming home for dinner," I told Amanda over my cell.

"Where are you eating?"

"At a friend's."

"Who?"

"Don't worry about it."

"I'm not worried. I just need to know what to say when Dad asks where you are."

"Tell him I wanted to work with someone from my math and English classes."

"Okay. And what's her name?"

How did she know? "Never mind."

"Be careful," Amanda said.

"I'll try."

When we got close to Lydia's house, I asked her, "Is your brother going to be there?"

"Of course. He's always there."

"Why?"

"He has to stay home. I told you."

"You didn't tell me anything. Why does he have to?"

"It's one of the conditions of his parole. He can't leave. House arrest."

"What?" I stopped walking. "Why is he under house arrest?"

"Oh, it was this whole thing where we lived before. He didn't actually kill anyone, if that's what you're thinking. You should see the look on your face. No, the guy can even kind of walk now, we heard. I'm sure I told you about this."

"Uh, no. I would remember."

"Well, don't worry about that. I really believe he wouldn't do anything like that again. Just be nice and don't get him mad. But don't take crap from him either, or he'll think you're patronizing him. That gets him really furious."

The living room was dark except for the flickering blue light from the TV. I could just see the back of her brother's head over the top of the couch. Lydia hit the light switch in the kitchen. The light flickered about a hundred times before it finally took.

Lydia rooted around in the refrigerator. "What do you feel like?" she asked.

"It doesn't matter. I'm not that hungry."

"I invited you for dinner. I'm gonna make you something." She closed the door and opened the freezer.

Frosty air blew out and swirled around her face like ghosts.

"Ah, the famous actors," a female voice said behind me. I turned. Standing there in what looked like a flight attendant's uniform was a near replica of Lydia. She was a little taller, had blond hair with dark roots, and was several years older, but other than that, she was practically a dead ringer. "Can I get your autographs?" she said.

"Hello, Gertrude," Lydia said.

"Why, good evening, Gertrude," the other person said.

"I thought you'd be at work."

"There was a delay. I'm on my way out."

"This is my sister, Maureen," Lydia said. "This is Ethan."

"How you doing?" I said.

"Just swell," Maureen Krane said. "You're even better looking than Lydia said you were."

I felt my face go hot.

"Forget it," Lydia said. She pulled some packages out of the freezer. "He's off-limits to you. Hands off." She ripped off the cellophane wrappers and stuck the things on plates and into the microwave.

"He is cute, though," Lydia's sister said. "I don't know if I can control myself." I started to get a weird fluttery feeling in my chest. I wanted to cough.

"Well, you're gonna have to. He's mine," Lydia said. "Go find someone your own age. Leave mine alone."

"Spoilsport," Maureen said. She made an exaggerated frown face and left.

Hold on. Rewind. Had Lydia just said "he's mine"?

The microwave beeped, and Lydia took out the two plates. She handed one to me. I wasn't totally sure what the steaming red, white, and yellow lumpy mess was supposed to be.

"Don't look like that," she said. "I said I would feed you. I never said it would be gourmet."

"What's that stink?" Lydia's brother called from the living room.

"Oh, the dead speaks. It's tamales, and no, you can't have any." She slung her backpack over her shoulder, took two forks out of the drawer, handed me a can of Coke, and nodded toward the stairs.

"Hey!"

I almost dropped my plate. I looked over. Her brother was turned around on the couch, peering at me.

"I remember you," he said. "You're that guy. You were here before."

"Right. How are you doing?"

"Going up, huh? Taking your hot tamales, are you? No hanky-panky, got it? Or I'll have to give you a little spanky." He clapped his hands together. It made me jump.

"Shut up, Ryan. Don't be an ass. Come on, Ethan."

She closed the door when we got to her room. First thing she did after putting her plate down, she unzipped her backpack and took something out. Her back was to me, but I saw a flash of green and knew it was that journal. She slipped it under her mattress in one smooth move, so I almost wouldn't have been able to notice.

"Your sister looks exactly like you," I said.

"Who?"

"Your sister?"

"Oh, right. Yeah. Like twins, right?"

"Really. What's that Gertrude stuff?"

"Oh. That's just something we do. Like an inside joke."

"How many years apart are you?"

Lydia laughed a little to herself. "She's not my sister. She's my mother."

"What? That was your mother? Why'd you say she was your sister?"

"But I was simply joking, my dear," she said, in the British accent.

"Wait. You're not going to tell me that the guy on the couch is really your father, are you?"

"He's my brother."

"So what about your dad?" I asked.

"Active service in the navy. He's somewhere in the Baltic Sea right now. Aren't you going to eat that?"

I looked at the tamale on my plate, and I wasn't sure if I could get it down.

"Not hungry?" Lydia said.

"Not totally."

"Me neither." She tilted her plate over the plastic wastebasket and waited until the mess broke its seal and slowly crawled down the plate, hung on the edge, and finally dropped into the garbage. I swallowed back my nausea.

"Here, give me your plate," she said.

"That's okay," I said. I put it on her desk. I couldn't watch that show again.

She looked at me for a moment, then said suddenly, "Be right back," and she was out of the room. I didn't know what to do, so I started to go to her small desk, to look at the designs and words covering her blotter. Something squished under my foot. I looked down. It was underwear. It's embarrassing to admit, but I bent down and picked it up. It was barely there, so tiny. It was a thong, which I'd never seen close up before. I couldn't imagine Jane wearing a thong; it was so not her style. She was basically pretty straight. No surprises.

But Lydia was one surprise after another. I knew pretty much everything about Jane, but with Lydia, I had no idea where the limits were. In fact, I wasn't sure if there even were limits. Everything was open. Anything could happen.

"You like my underwear?"

I spun around. There she was. And I was standing there with her thong in my hand like some kind of pervert. Just kill me now.

"It's okay. You don't have to blush. Have you been in

many girls' bedrooms?" she whispered in a deep voice.

"Uh. No." I cleared my throat again to cover that my breathing was coming a little faster.

She was standing close. She held my closed hands in hers.

"Do you like being in my bedroom?"

"Yeah," I said.

"I've been waiting for this to happen."

"Me, too."

She closed her eyes. I put my hands on her hips, lightly. I was nervous, electric.

"What do you want to do?" she said.

"I want . . ."

"Tell me."

"I want . . ." I didn't know how to say it.

"Do you want it more than anything?" Her lips brushed mine as she whispered.

"Yes."

"Would you do anything to get it?"

I breathed out. I couldn't speak.

She dropped her head back, her eyes closed, her lips barely parted, ready.

I leaned forward, my mouth to hers.

And just before our lips touched, she slipped out of my arms and was across the room.

"That was really good," she said.

"Huh?" I said.

"Very realistic. I believed you really felt it."

"I did."

"Well, that's good. You can use that. When you feel it for real, that's good. That's what acting is all about."

I swallowed. She was looking me right in the eyes, and I realized I had no idea if she was acting when she didn't want me, or acting when she did.

◈ ◈

When I got home, Mom was sitting at the kitchen table, Dad was standing by her, and I knew something was up from their serious faces.

"We've been waiting for you," Mom said.

"I called. I told Amanda I'd be late."

"Well, we've been waiting to talk to you about something that came in the mail today."

"What?"

"Your report card."

Gulp. "My report card should be good."

"Well, English, social studies, they were fine, all A-minuses," Dad said. "Perfectly acceptable."

"Though we both believe you could do better."

"I'm trying."

"You did end up with a B-plus in math, which is a disappointment. But that isn't what we wanted to talk about."

"Okay. What is it?"

"Chemistry," Mom said.

Double gulp. He backed out of the deal. I knew he would. That time he talked to me in the hall, I knew then that he wasn't going to go through with it, that he was too disgusted with me and he was going to take his chances with Lydia.

"An A."

"What?"

"You got an A in chemistry!" Mom said with a big grin.

"Now you see that?" Dad said. He grabbed my shoulder and jostled me. "You see? We could tell that you didn't feel confident in chemistry, but see what happens when you apply yourself? An A!"

"You've shown us—and yourself—the kind of stuff you're really made of. Chemistry is a tough subject, and you came through with flying colors." Mom actually hugged me. She whispered in my ear, "I'm very proud of you."

Great. Now stab me in the heart, why don't you?

They were right about one thing, though. I had shown myself the stuff I was truly made of.

✞ ✞

"Come in here a minute," Amanda said.

I went into her room. She was sitting at her computer. "How did you get an A in honors chem?"

"What do you mean, how? I just did."

She looked at me, watching my face. It was hard to lie to Amanda. And I remembered what Jane had said about the twitch at my eye when I lied. I didn't know if Amanda knew about that, but I rubbed my eyes like I was tired, just to make sure. I picked up a CD case on her desk and worked on actually memorizing the order of songs on the back. That's what we call stage business. And I did have a motivation: not to get caught lying.

"Honors chem is the hardest science course we have. I had to grind to get an A-minus, and, no offense, but I happen to be better than you at science. So how did you pull off a flat A?"

I shrugged.

"Come on, I'm curious. Just tell me the truth."

"Okay. I blackmailed the teacher, and he had no choice but to give me an A."

"Fine. Don't tell me. Anyway, congratulations. That's pretty impressive."

"Thanks." I started to leave.

"Hey. One other thing. What's happening with you and Jane?"

"Why?"

"Did you break up with her?"

"Why are you asking me that?"

"Because Sharon Althouse's brother hangs out with Jane's brother, and word got back to me that you broke up with her. Is it true?"

"Well, no. I guess she broke up with me."

"You're an idiot."

"How can I be the idiot if *she* broke up with *me*?"

"Because you did something you shouldn't have. You must have. She was crazy about you, and you must have done something pretty bad for her to want to break up."

"So it's all my fault."

"Probably."

I put my hands up, like, what am I supposed to say to that?

"So you did become that kind of guy," Amanda said. She shook her head.

I shook my head. But I had to wonder if maybe she was right.

LOOSE

I waited outside the cafeteria to intercept Jane. I saw her coming with the crowd, talking to Nora. Scott and Tim were trailing right behind. I got a nervous fluttery feeling. I'd never, ever felt nervous around Jane before.

She slowed a little bit when she saw me standing there. She looked a little confused, like maybe she was trying to figure out what I wanted.

"Hi," she said quietly.

"Hey, Ethan," Scott said. Nora gave me a half smile and pretended to look for something in her backpack.

"Can I talk to you for a minute?" I said to Jane.

"Are you coming back to sit with us?" Tim asked.

"I don't know. I just need to talk to Jane."

"Just go ahead," Jane said to them. "Can you get me some fries? And a wrap?" She handed some money to Nora, who grabbed Tim by the handle on the back of his bag and pulled him away.

"Listen," I said. "I'm kind of uncomfortable about how we left things."

"No kidding? You're uncomfortable. Well, then,

maybe I should just wait for you while you have your fun with every girl in town."

"What the hell are you talking about? Are you kidding me?"

"You're uncomfortable? How do you think I felt, with you running around with that girl?" She glared at me.

I was stuck between wanting to apologize and just being pissed off that she was being so harsh and cold.

"Let me explain something," I said. "What you thought was happening with me and her. It wasn't happening."

"Oh, please."

"I'm telling you."

"Jordan told me all about it."

"Jordan Paul Whiting, you mean? What are you talking to that jerk for?"

"First of all, he's not the jerk you always made him out to be. He's actually very sweet."

"Sweet? Oh, wait, I was confused. See, I thought we were talking about Jordan Paul Whiting."

"Be sarcastic all you want. At least he's honest with me."

"Hold on one second. Since when do you spend time with him?"

"You know he's in my social studies class. And I hang with him now. He's nice to me. Nicer than you were. He told me all about you and Lydia Krane. How you look at each other and giggle together, and come and go with each other. So I can understand why you don't like him. He told me the truth about you."

"He told you a bunch of crap."

"And you know what? I'm grateful to him for helping me see what you're really about." I had never heard her talk to me in such an icy, vicious tone.

"You know what, Jane? Whatever."

"That's right. Whatever."

She turned and walked into the caf. And as I watched her go, I shivered, as if it was frigid air she had left behind. And I thought for the very first time, maybe I'm better off without her.

❧ ❧

The next period after lunch was chemistry, and I spent the whole period wondering what had happened between Jane and me. Okay, there was no point in denying that I had been kind of infatuated with Lydia while I was with Jane, but I hadn't really done anything. So how is it fair that I get convicted for something I hadn't even done yet?

I sensed a quiet come over the class. I looked up. Mr. Dugan had stopped lecturing. He was looking at me. What? What's the problem? As if he could tell what I thought, he shook his head and went back to his deathly boring description of the combined gas law formula. Big yawn. Like that was going to be really important for me to know in my life. I turned back to the window.

I could start to see now, Jane wasn't perfect either.

She really was kind of rigid, and though it bothered me when Lydia used to call Jane my wife, maybe she wasn't so far off. Maybe we had settled into this boring routine. One thing about Lydia: she wasn't routine. She might have been a little bit strange, and I was still probably a little bit scared of the way she got people to do things that she wanted them to do, but she was definitely interesting.

The bell rang. I gathered up my stuff and followed everyone out.

"Lederer," Mr. Dugan called. I turned. He stepped out in the hall with me, like before. But there was this cold anger in his eyes.

"I got a call from your father. He said, 'Thanks for being such a good teacher. Ethan would not have been able to get such a high grade in honors chemistry without your fine instruction and generous help.' I was disgusted. Smugness must run in the family."

"Now hold on one minute. He doesn't know anything."

"And there you are, sitting in my class, daydreaming the period away, so confident. What if I just change my mind, decide to give you the marks you deserve, and take my chances with your false accusations?"

"Go ahead."

"Really? What a show of courage. But I know you'll lie and cheat and do whatever you can to make sure you get what you want. That's quite a sense of integrity you have. Your father apparently taught you well. I'm sure the apple doesn't fall far from the tree."

That was it. That expression "Something snapped in me" is really true. Maybe it was just a crick in my neck, but when I stepped in close to him, I actually heard a snap, like a stick breaking.

"Okay," I said. "You're right. I'm not good in chemistry. But I am pretty smart. And more important, I am determined. You don't know my father, so I'd appreciate it if you wouldn't talk about him. And you don't know me, either. You don't know what I might do. It's our word against yours. We won't stop until you are ruined. Consider that a promise."

I noticed then that he had backed up against the lockers, and I was leaning in close to him.

I hadn't gotten into a fight since first grade, and I hardly considered myself physically threatening. But I felt at that moment that if he touched me or said one more thing about me or my family, I could go ballistic.

Lydia was right. Once you start playing the part and you believe in it, it becomes true.

❧ ❧

I was trying to figure out what I should say to Jordan Paul at rehearsal about his telling Jane that I was involved with Lydia, but it turned out that he wasn't at rehearsal because he wasn't in any of the scenes we were working on. Neither was Lydia. We did a bunch of scenes between my character and the Three Ingénues, who were played by three of the DramaRamas and had the same purpose as the

Three Witches in *Macbeth*. They predicted the future and commented on the action, but in our version, they weren't witches, they were Scientologists.

After rehearsal, I headed home by myself, but when I got to the pond, I saw Lydia. She was sitting with her back against a tree, writing in that green journal. I watched her for a little while without her knowing.

There she was, writing, writing, her hair fallen over her face. It was hard to believe that barely a month ago, I didn't even know her, didn't even know she existed. Then she came into my life, and everything was different. She knew me, understood me, better than any of the people I had known for so long.

"How long are you just going to stare at me?" she said.

"I didn't know you saw me here."

"I don't need to see you to know when you're near me." She closed her journal and pushed it deep inside her backpack. I went over and dropped my bag next to her.

"How was rehearsal?" she asked.

"Okay. Kind of amateur hour without you there."

She stood up and brushed off the seat of her pants. "Let's go out and get a bagel or something."

We ran our lines while we walked. We went to Benny J's, the better bagel shop in town. I hadn't ever been in town with Lydia before, and I kept an eye out for people I knew. Even though Jane and I were done, it still would have felt awkward if I ran into her with Lydia. But nobody I knew was at Benny J's. It was pretty crowded with mostly older kids and parents.

We finished our bagels and went back to running lines at the table.

"I'm sick of all the no-talent, flash-in-the-pan Hollywood brats leaping ahead of us, taking our roles," she said. "We're going to be king and queen of this town before we're done." Lydia said it kind of loud, and a woman on line gave her a look.

"Sssh," I said.

"Sssh, what?"

"You're being a little loud."

"So?"

"People are looking at us."

"And?"

"I'm just saying. We can do this without disturbing them."

Lydia looked at me and smiled. "You really need to get over that."

"Get over what?"

"Why are you so worried about disturbing other people?"

"What?"

"We're acting. We can be as disturbing as we need to be," she said, making her voice even louder. "That's called art."

"Well, maybe they'll think we're disturbed," I said. Try to make a joke of it. Don't let her make a scene.

"We're disturbed!" she said loudly. Some more people looked at her.

"Stop," I said. I smiled, but I was getting nervous.

"You worry too much about what other people think. You need to loosen up. Be silly, funny, scary, loud, stupid, ugly."

"I'm loose enough."

"Yeah, right. Let go. Get wild," she said, being loud again.

"It's hard to let go."

"It's not hard. Just do it." I knew in theory that she was right. But I just couldn't be that way. She watched me.

"I'm about to embarrass you," she said.

"What? Don't."

"Better get with it, or I'll make the biggest scene you've ever seen."

"Lydia?"

She smiled at me, raised her eyebrows, then her face changed into a mask of anger. "I am so sick of catching you looking at those kind of magazines! What is wrong with you?" she said really loudly. "I mean, are you sick?"

Along with about half the people in the store, I stared at her. She looked at me with a horrified expression.

"Is it a sickness or something that makes you look at them? Are you some kind of a *perv* or something?"

I was stunned. "You're very, very loud," I said slowly in a whisper. I wanted to disappear.

"You have no idea," she said quietly. Then, loud again. "Maybe you need to see a doctor or something. Because I think you're a sick, sick person!"

It felt like every person in the shop was staring at us. I wouldn't know, since I was afraid to look around. My eyes were glued to Lydia, trying telepathically to get her to stop. But I knew better. She was just getting warmed up.

"Only a desperate, creepy loser would look at that stuff. Is that what you are? A loser?" She practically shouted it. And then she kicked me hard under the table.

"Maybe I wouldn't need to look at them if you wouldn't keep getting pregnant!" I shouted back at her. What? I took a breath, but before I could tell myself to shut up, I banged the table. "I mean, this is the fourth time!"

Lydia's mouth just about dropped open, but she caught herself. "Are you kidding me? Is that what this is about?"

"Yeah. I mean, what I am supposed to do? With the first one, you forced me to get married. You keep insisting on getting knocked up."

"Well, maybe I want some company while you're at school."

"Maybe if you'd stop having babies, *you* could go back and finish middle school!"

Lydia stared at me. I got her. I knew every single person was staring at us, and I didn't even care. The owner guy, wearing an apron and with flour on his neck, came over to us.

"Listen. You kids need to take this outside."

"He's a total pervert," Lydia said loudly to the guy.

"She's fifteen and on her second marriage!"

"I don't know about any of that, but you're disturbing the other customers. Please leave."

"We're trying to work out our problems," Lydia shouted.

"Don't you have any sense of romance?" I asked.

"Yeah, well, go be romantic outside, kids. Don't make me call the police."

Lydia and I looked at each other, got up, and went to the door. Just before we went through, I turned back toward the inside. Like I guessed, everyone was watching me. I looked at the owner. "Don't worry. We'll work it out. And next time we'll bring the kids."

I couldn't stop grinning when I got outside. I felt like I'd passed some really important test or something. I felt free.

Lydia smiled at me and shook her head. "Well, look at that," she said.

"How's that for loose?"

BURN

I was walking in the hall before lunch, and I saw something that just made me stop in my tracks. It was pretty far down the hall, so I couldn't be 100 percent sure, but I was almost certain. It looked like Jane walking with Jordan Paul Whiting, and from where I was standing, it looked like they were holding hands.

I can't believe it. I can't believe it. I kept saying it over and over to myself. I just can't believe it.

How could she do that? Just to get back at me, she picked a guy who was practically brain-dead and a total jerk besides? Was Jane really that shallow, that she would go with someone like him, a guy she knew I didn't like or respect, all just to get back at me? I kept trying to tell myself that maybe it was the real Jane after all, maybe I thought there was more to her than there really was. That had to be true if she would go out with Jordan Paul Whiting.

But as much as I tried to look at it like they deserved each other, or like it was a good thing that I found this out about Jane, I have to say that it really got to me. It was like a splinter that breaks off and leaves a piece buried in your skin. You can see it through the layers, but you can't get it.

I went to the library at lunch, as usual. I pulled a book of photography from the shelf, but I couldn't even concentrate on the pictures.

Why would she go out with him? Why would she do that? The questions kept repeating themselves in my head, and I couldn't stop them.

I felt something touch the edge of my ear and I jumped. It was Lydia, touching me with her finger. She laughed.

"It's not funny," I said. "You totally scared me."

"Easy, boy," she said in a Scottish accent. "Let's you just take it easy, laddie."

"Come on. Just don't sneak up on me like that."

"You need to relax," she said, switching to her Southern accent. "What's wrong with you?"

"Nothing. I'm just . . . I have stuff on my mind."

She put her hands on my shoulders and squeezed. "You are just wound *way* too tight. Come on. We're going on an adventure."

"I don't like the sound of that."

"Oh, but you will. Come on." She grinned at me and winked.

I followed her. She went out into the hall. I looked both ways, up toward the principal's office, and down the other way toward guidance.

"Oh, come on," Lydia said. "Don't be such a coward. *Act* brave and you *are* brave."

I followed her into the hallway. She stopped at my locker and opened it. "How do you know my combination?" I asked.

"I know a lot of things," she said. She handed me my jacket.

"We can't go out anywhere. We're sophomores. And besides, there's still a full afternoon of school."

"For them, maybe."

"Hold on. I don't cut."

"You're such a rule follower."

I looked in her eyes. "So where are you taking me, anyway? Another public performance in the bagel store?"

"No, that's done. This is better."

"What is it?"

She smiled, leaned in, and whispered in my ear in that way that made me melt. "You'll have to trust me," she said.

❧ ❧

We blew out a back door, ran like commandos into the woods, and came out the other side near the downtown area.

She took me through the seedy part of town. This was a place none of us went. There was a house that leaned about twenty degrees to the left. Next door, there was a house with a sagging roof that looked like a collapsed soufflé. The porch was covered with huge, thick curls of peeled paint.

"Do you have some kind of destination in mind, or are we just here to take in the scenery?" I asked.

She didn't say anything. She just took my hand and kept walking. She'd been right about cutting loose the other day in the bagel store. I was pretty curious about what she had planned this time.

We took a couple of more turns and headed down a hill toward the highway. Right before the exit, she stopped in front of a small white building. There were three Harleys parked out front. Hanging in the window was a neon sign that read:

TATTOOS
and
PIERCINGS

"Oh, no, no, no," I said. "Forget it."

She smiled at me.

"Are we here for you?" I said. "Because I can tell you one thing, we're not here for *me*. I am not getting any part of me pierced. Forget it."

"I didn't mention anything about you getting a piercing, did I? Although, now that you mention it—"

"Not a chance."

She laughed. "Come on." She pulled me toward the door.

"I don't want to."

"Stop being a little wuss. Just come inside."

"We're here for you, right?" I said.

"Okay, fine. We're here for me. Now come on."

She pulled me in and shut the door behind us. There were voices coming from a back room.

"Be right out," came a male voice.

"Sounds good," Lydia called.

"No rush," I added.

I looked at the walls. They were covered with logos, pictures, symbols, tribal designs, and cartoon figures that were cute/scary. It was like a museum dedicated to bad taste.

"Isn't this one a riot?" Lydia said. She pointed to a cartoon demon with a leering grin, clutching a pitchfork between his chubby bright red legs. The caption underneath read: Horny Devil.

"Yeah," I said. "It's very classy."

"How about this one?" She pointed to a skull gripping a long-stemmed rose between its teeth, flames coming from behind its top hat.

"You know, it looks familiar. Isn't that based on a da Vinci painting?"

I started to relax as we walked around, looking and joking about the snoozing hillbilly, the two-gunned bandito, the religious figures who looked more drunk than holy.

After a while, two people came out of the back room. They were both built like beer kegs with legs. They wore black T-shirts and leather vests, jeans with chains looping

from pockets. I was pretty sure one was male, based on
the long thick beard. The other was probably female, but
I wouldn't have bet too much money on it. Their arms
were covered with red and green and black and orange
and yellow. Each of them had a piece of clean gauze taped
to their upper arms, probably covering fresh his-and-hers
tattoos.

They looked totally in love as they walked past us and
out the door.

"That was kind of weird," I said.

"Not for a place like this."

"Have you spent a lot of time in places like this?"

Before she could answer, a guy came out, wiping his
hands on a towel. He was tall and thin, wearing a black
tank top. His arms and neck were covered with tattoos.
His ears had multiple piercings, running all the way along
the outer edge. He also had what looked like a tiny silver
arrow stuck through his eyebrow, and a bolt coming out
of his lower lip.

He looked at us and shook his head.

"Sorry, guys. You have to be eighteen. State law."

"How do you know we're not eighteen?" Lydia said
with that smile.

"Gimme a break," the guy said, giving her back a
smile. It was not as sweet and alluring as Lydia's, mostly
due to the fact that the guy had gotten his teeth filed into
fangs.

"It's not like I don't already have ink," Lydia said. She

rolled up her sleeves. The guy laughed at her. "Some of this is real," she said. "Give me some cotton and alcohol, I'll show you."

He held a piece of gauze to the mouth of a gray bottle and upended it. He handed her the soaked gauze. She scrubbed at her arm. A lot of the designs came off, but a few stayed. One was a ring of thorns around her upper arm. Another was the anarchist's A in a circle. There was also a bloody rose.

The guy seemed pretty unimpressed.

"Not bad work. But it doesn't change anything. I can't help you."

"It's okay. We didn't want anything anyway," I said.

Lydia gave me a look, then turned back to him. "My name's Lydia. Can I talk to you for a second?" She nodded toward the back room.

"My name's Randall. And you can talk all you want, honey. It's still gonna be no-go. I'm not losing my license."

She smiled and went into the back room with the guy. I heard them talking, but I couldn't make out the words at all. The last time Lydia went off and left me waiting for her, we ended up blackmailing a teacher. I hoped nothing like that was going on in the next room. After a few minutes, they came out.

"I don't do anything on the face, and I don't do anything on the hands," he said. He walked to the door and flipped the sign, so it read: CLOSED. "So who's first?"

As we walked through the curtain into the back room,

I asked Lydia, "Did you threaten this guy or what?"

"Please."

"Why did he agree to give you a tattoo if you're underage?"

"Money talks, baby."

"You're crazy. But don't think just because you're getting one, that I am, too."

Twenty minutes later, Lydia was straddling the bench, leaning forward against the backrest, hugging it. Randall had her hair clipped up on top of her head. He had a silvery apparatus attached to his hand, and he worked slowly, filling in a rising golden sun on the back of Lydia's neck. Every couple of seconds, he wiped her neck with a piece of gauze. I wasn't sure if it was ink or blood he was wiping away, and I didn't want to know.

I was sitting down and leaning back in a chair because I had gotten queasy as soon as he had started on Lydia. Finally the guy finished and wiped it off a few more times. Lydia sat up and he handed her a mirror. She looked at the reflection of a reflection in the big mirror.

"Very nice," she said. "Thanks."

"Okay, big guy. You're next."

"Oh no, I'm not."

"Give us a minute, okay, Randall?" Randall shrugged, and Lydia grabbed my arm and pulled me to the wall.

"Don't be a baby. It's not a big deal."

"I'm not getting a tattoo."

"Just a little one. So you know you broke through a

barrier. So you know you have the guts not to be a drone, a little rule follower, all your life."

"I can't."

"Yes, you can. Look." She pointed at a bunch of Asian characters. "Just get one of these."

I had to admit, they looked kind of cool. And like always, Lydia could read me like a book.

"Here's what I'm thinking," she said. "We'll get one that says 'courage.' Just a few tiny characters on the back of your shoulder. Very cool."

"I don't have any money."

"I already paid him."

"It hurts, right?"

"Some, but that's okay. Pain passes. And then you have courage for the rest of your life."

I didn't say anything for a minute. But maybe this wasn't the worst idea. I mean, I was starting to change, to open up, to take chances in my life. Why not just get it and, as she said, have courage for the rest of my life?

"Very little, though," I said.

"Good boy. Take your shirt off and lie down on that bench. I'll go talk to him. I'll make sure he keeps it small."

Lydia held my hand while he worked on me. It definitely hurt, more than a little. The whole area where he was working felt like he was jabbing a fine soldering iron into the worst sunburn imaginable. And add to that the burn when he wiped the blood away with gauze that felt like sandpaper. But Lydia was right. Pain passes, and I felt that I was moving through something by doing this and getting past the pain.

Was I actually getting a tattoo? As Mom would have said, what had gotten into me? Lydia had some kind of power over me. It seemed like she could get me to do just about anything.

But I knew that wasn't really true. Lydia was helping me to see things about myself. But I was making decisions that were mine to make. I was being who I wanted to be.

∽ ∾

At home in the bathroom that night, I tried to get a good look over my shoulder in the mirror. I had untaped the top half of the gauze and was having a hard time seeing it. I opened the medicine cabinet and angled it so I could see a reflection of a reflection of a reflection of myself.

The tattoo didn't look so great. It was inflamed and shiny from the Bacitracin ointment I had just put on. But that was what Randall said it would look like for a while, until all the dead skin sheds. That sounded really pleasant.

Obviously I couldn't tell anyone at home about it. But I was glad that I'd gone ahead and gotten it. I had been starting to feel different lately. And the tattoo was part of the new me.

There was a knock on the door. "Hey. There's a phone call for you," Amanda said.

"Who is it?"

"Lydia?"

"Oh. Okay. I'm coming." I tried to hurry up and get the gauze taped back, and my shirt on. I unlocked the door and pulled it open.

"Finally," Amanda said. "I've been waiting forty minutes to take a shower." She handed me the cordless phone. I took it into my room.

"Hi," I said.

"Let me guess. You pulled the gauze off and were looking at it."

"Not at all."

"I know you're lying. Do you like it?"

"It doesn't look so good right now."

"It will. It's going to be so cool."

"Well, I am glad I got it. What are you doing?"

"Lying around. And thinking about you," she said.

"Really?"

"Of course. I think about you all the time. Especially in bed, right before I go to sleep."

"Really?"

"Always. When do you think of me?"

"To tell the truth, pretty much all the time," I said.

"That's good. That's what I was hoping you'd say. It's true, though, right?"

"It's true."

"I would know if you lied to me."

"I'm not lying."

"Don't ever lie to me." There was kind of a weird tone

to her voice, one that I never heard.

"I wouldn't."

"Good." She didn't say anything for a couple of seconds. When she spoke again, it was in her Southern accent. "I have a question for you. How come you never invited me over to your house?"

"Over here? I don't know."

"You aren't ashamed of me or anything, are you?"

"Are you kidding?"

"That's not a no."

"No, no. I am not ashamed of you. At all. Why don't you come over tomorrow after rehearsal?" I said.

"Really?"

"Sure. Why not?"

A little while later, I mentioned to Mom that I wanted to have a friend over for dinner the next night.

"Who, Jane?"

"No. It's someone else. She's in my classes. Oh, and the play."

Mom watched me and nodded. "Okay," she said.

ঌ ঌ

Tim caught me in the hallway.

"We never see you anymore," he said. "Are you coming back?"

"I don't know. It's pretty awkward, with Jane and everything."

"Yeah, I guess." Tim wasn't great at keeping eye contact when he was nervous or uncomfortable. He was looking straight down at my feet. "Are you hooked up with that girl?" he asked.

"Lydia. Yeah. I think."

"You think? You don't know if you are or not?"

"It's kind of complicated."

He nodded like he understood, but I knew he didn't.

"I don't like that Jordan guy," Tim said.

"What? What do you mean?"

"I mean he's kind of not so nice. I don't really like him."

"Wait a second. Are you telling me that Jane is going out with him?"

Tim looked up at me, then back down again. "You know, you should probably ask her."

"Well I'm asking you."

"I guess she's going out with him."

"You have got to be kidding!"

"Kind of the same way you're going out with that girl. In a complicated way."

I looked at Tim. I couldn't remember him ever being sarcastic or sharp before.

I brooded about the idea of Jane and Jordan all afternoon. Clearly, this whole thing was about me, and their little plot to get revenge. And if that's what they wanted to do, then fine with me.

Most of rehearsal was devoted to having the film/video team record certain parts that were going to be used on the screens for the film-within-the play scenes. We didn't totally understand how this stuff was all going to work, but Mr. Lombardi had some plan. After they were done filming us, we got into the regular part of the rehearsal. One of the DramaRamas still hadn't learned the ten lines she had, and Mr. Lombardi got upset.

"Sorry," she said. "I'll learn them. It's no big deal. I'm just a small part anyway."

"Haven't you people ever heard the expression 'There are no small parts, only small actors'?"

"That's a lie," Jordan Paul said.

Whoa. Jordan Paul had never argued with Mr. Lombardi before. He always nodded knowingly at whatever Mr. Lombardi said, whether he understood it or not. So this was pretty big.

"It's a lie?"

"Some parts are smaller than others. It's a fact."

"They may have fewer lines, but they're not smaller. Not to the character."

He stood up and put his script notebook on the chair. "No character thinks he or she is small. They all think they're the center and the other people are the supporting characters. Tom Stoppard wrote a play where Rosencrantz and Guildenstern think they're the main characters and Hamlet is a small, supporting character. And to them, it's true. They're the center. It's just like life."

"How?" asked Bridget Pierce.

"How? Are you the center of your life, or are you

simply around to be a supporting character in somebody else's life? Who's the lead, who's the star, you or her?" he asked, pointing to Kathy Michaels.

"I'm the star, of course," Bridget said, tossing her hair in movie star fashion, and getting the laugh she wanted from everyone.

"Ah. But to her, *she's* the star and you're just a walk-on. Don't you see that? It needs to be like that for your characters, because it's like that in life, for all of us."

✎ ✎

"I like what he was saying to us, about how everyone is the center of their own story," I said to Lydia as we walked to my house.

"Well, of course."

"I just hadn't really thought of it that way." It was getting dark earlier, and the temperature was dropping. I had worn the wrong jacket and was feeling cold.

"I like that he connected it to life," she said. "Too many people don't see that life and drama are connected. Or should be."

"Shouldn't they be separate?" I asked.

"Why?"

"Because if you can't separate drama from reality, then isn't that what's usually called crazy?"

"Well, no. I mean, definitely, acting has to be a choice, something you do on purpose. But if you can switch back and forth between acting a character and being yourself, then your acting is better, and your life is better. I go back and forth all the time."

I nodded. My back was aching from clenching against the cold.

"You know, my dear boy, I really must confess something to you." She was laying on the Southern accent thicker than she ever had. She sounded like she was Scarlet O'Hara in *Gone with the Wind*.

"Why, let's have it, my dear," I said, trying to sound like Rhett Butler, but probably sounding more like someone with an adenoid problem.

"Well, the truth of the matter is that I am deeply and passionately and hopelessly in love with you. And I surely don't mean some schoolgirl crush, or a passing fancy. What I mean is that I do love with all my heart and all my soul."

"My buttercup, the feeling is mutual, I assure you," I said.

"My sweetest, you may think I am merely playacting, but I assure you, I am not. You are everything to me, and I would simply wither away if you were ever to leave me, or love another woman."

"You need have no fear of that, my darling. You are the only woman I will ever love. Forever and evermore."

"Swear it," she said.

"I do swear it."

She let out a dramatic sigh and took my arm.

As we walked in silence, I was dying to know how much of what she said was acting and how much was real.

WEIRD FOR ME

"So how long have you lived in West Baring, Lydia?" Mom asked.

"We moved in about a month ago." Lydia wasn't speaking with any kind of accent at all. Just her plain voice.

"How do you like it here?" Dad asked.

"Oh, it's fine." She had been very quiet, barely speaking since we walked in and sat down to dinner. Mom had made some kind of chicken with wild mushrooms that looked a little funky, but it was actually okay. Mom and Dad and Amanda were all acting totally normal and nice, but something was up with Lydia. She was completely shy and basically not acting like herself.

"Where did you live before here?" Mom asked.

Lydia looked at her plate and took a breath.

"Why is everyone interrogating her?" I said.

"We're not interrogating her," Dad said. "We're just trying to get to know her. We certainly didn't mean to make you uncomfortable, Lydia, if we're asking too many questions."

"No, it's okay. We lived in Pennsylvania before here."

Mom was about to ask something, probably where in Pennsylvania, but I gave her a look, and she backed off. Instead, she turned to Amanda. "So, you were telling me about that problem with the yearbook team."

And from there we steered the conversation away from Lydia and kept it away from her. I watched her during dinner. She didn't say another word, and out of politeness, tried to look at whoever was talking, but I could see that she was barely there.

When dinner was over, I said, "So you want to study some of that stuff for math?"

"Well, you know, I would, but I really should go home. It's kind of late."

"Really? Okay. I'll walk you."

"I'll take you guys," Amanda said.

Except for Lydia's directions, the car was silent on the five-minute ride to her house.

"This is it," she said when we got there. "Thanks for the ride. And thank your parents again for dinner."

"Good to meet you. Take care," Amanda said.

"I'll be right back," I said, and I followed Lydia out.

I touched her arm when we got to her front door. "Are you okay?"

"Fine."

"You were totally quiet all night. I was wondering."

"Well, it was pretty weird for me."

It was weird for her? With that brother of hers, and

the mother who they pretend is her sister? "Weird how?"

"Well, it was basically like stepping into one of those shows they have on Nick at Nite or something. *Leave It to Beaver*, or *Ozzie and Harriet*, or whatever."

"Oh."

"I mean, very nice and all that. Don't get me wrong. But God."

I nodded. "I guess I know what you mean." I did, and I didn't.

"Well, anyway. It's good I got to meet them. It helps me understand what happened to you, to make you the way you are."

"That's true."

"It was very disturbing," she said.

"Disturbing?"

"Sure. That whole aren't-we-perfect, the plastic-all-American thing?"

"Well, I guess now you get what I've been talking about."

"I get it. It was actually kind of creepy. No offense."

It always amazes me how people say no offense right after saying something offensive, like that erases it. But I didn't know what to say and I felt a little like I'd betrayed my family by not defending them.

"So, I'll see you tomorrow," she said.

"Yeah." I thought of leaning in to kiss her, but Amanda was right there in the car, and we hadn't really done that yet. All in all, it was a very awkward moment.

When the front door closed quietly behind Lydia, I got back in the car. Amanda opened her mouth to speak.

"Don't say it," I said.

"What?"

"Anything. Whatever you're going to say."

"I wasn't going to say a thing."

"Good."

She turned the corner. "But she sure doesn't say much."

"She was nervous. Shy. She's not usually like that."

"Really? What is she usually like?"

"Not like that. Let's just let it go."

"Okay." We were quiet until we pulled into the garage. Amanda turned to me. "That's the girl you broke up with Jane for?"

"Can you please just not ask me any questions about this? Please?"

"Okay. Fine."

I opened my car door.

"And I won't make any comments about how I think you made a really, really big mistake," Amanda said. "I won't say a thing."

≈ ≈

All morning, Lydia totally avoided eye contact with me in all our classes. She just wrote in that green journal and kept to herself. When the bell rang, she hurried out of class before I could even get to her.

After fifth-period history, I saw Jane standing by her

locker. She was just standing there, thinking about something. I thought about going over to her, though I didn't know what I'd say. Still, I started to walk over. And that's when I saw Jordan Paul walking toward her. She smiled at him as he got closer. When he got there, he put his hands on her shoulders and kissed her, right in the hallway.

What? You idiot, don't you even know how much she doesn't like PDAs? Don't you know how much she hates that?

But she didn't look like she hated it. In fact, she smiled and kissed him back.

What? Don't you remember how much you don't like being kissed in public? Jane? What is this all about?

They held hands as they walked off down the hall and disappeared into the crowd.

I stood there, feeling like a jerk.

I went into the library for lunch period, and as soon as I walked in, I felt a hand on my arm, pulling me.

"Come here," Lydia said. No accent. She pulled me deep into the stacks.

"Are you okay?" I said. "You've been rushing out of class all day. I wanted to talk to you."

"Just come here."

"You've been acting kind of different since last night. I don't know what bothered you so much, but whatever it is, if I did something wrong, I'm sorry."

"Never mind that." She stopped walking in the middle

of the stacks. There was nobody around us. "I need to ask you something."

"Go ahead."

"You won't leave me, will you?"

"What?" I said.

"I just have this feeling you're going to leave me, dump me."

"Why would you think that?"

"I just do. Tell me you won't leave me."

"Lydia? What are you talking about?"

She looked at me. I was about to speak, but I didn't get a chance. She grabbed my face and kissed me.

Then she swung me around and back into the opposite bookshelf. I heard books falling to the floor. She had one foot behind my leg, one arm around my waist, the other locked around my neck. She was pulling me so tight to her that I thought of that Groucho Marx line, *If I hold you any closer, I'll be in back of you.* She was kissing me so furiously, I could barely breathe. I almost laughed.

She swung me back to the other side and more books fell. She pushed her face two inches away from mine and grabbed my hair. She glared at me, her eyes dark as rain clouds.

"Don't you leave me," she said.

And she hit me on the side of the face. Hard.

My mouth dropped open, and before I could say anything, she drove herself into me again, kissing me as if her life depended on it.

And then she was gone, leaving me with nothing but a pounding heart, a stinging eye, and a mind filled with confusion.

❧ ❧

When I got into the auditorium, hammer blows echoed like gunshots as the crew banged together pieces of wood to make the flats. Some of the art students were painting the ones that were already built. Some kids from the film/video club were setting up the screens and monitors that were going to show the rushes and film-within-the-play scenes. The day before, a girl and guy who were both going to a prestigious fashion institute next year came and took some measurements for the few costumes that needed to be made. Most of the play was going to be in modern Hollywood-style dress. But the scenes of the movie within the play were in pseudo-medieval costume. All of this meant that we were getting very close to the performances.

Mr. Lombardi was onstage with Jordan. It was going to be just us rehearsing.

"Today we're going to work on the final scene of Act Five," Mr. Lombardi said. "This is the part where Mike and Duffy finally battle it out under the Hollywood sign. This is the big climax, if you will. So today is your lesson in stage fencing. Safety is going to be our priority!"

When I got up on the stage, Mr. Lombardi handed each of us a long thin sword. It was a little thicker than a car antenna. "A thrust from this won't even hurt," Mr. Lombardi said. "Watch." He put the tip of my foil against his stomach. "Now push, Ethan." I did and the foil easily bent in a big curve. "These are made to be reflective so they can be seen from the audience, and, as you'll find, they make a nice loud noise when they clash, but they won't do any damage."

I looked over at Jordan Paul. He tested the foil in the air, slashing it back and forth so it made a loud swish sound. I whipped my foil through the air. The sound it made was straight out of Robin Hood. Pretty cool.

"The other part of our fight is the dagger." Mr. Lombardi picked up two glinting daggers off the stage. He turned, took a step, and tripped. He stumbled right at me. I dropped the foil and reached out to steady him. The dagger flashed and went straight into my arm.

I gasped and looked at Mr. Lombardi's grinning face. He held out the dagger and showed me how the blade slipped right into the dagger handle.

"Hold out your finger," he said. I held my hand out and he showed me how the tiniest pressure moved the fake blade into the handle. As he demonstrated it to Jordan Paul, I thought about that urban legend where there was a high school play of *Julius Caesar* and someone switched the rubber knives for real ones and the kid got stabbed. I had believed that story until I found out how many people had heard the same story, supposedly happening on about a thousand different high school stages.

"So you see that these props are totally safe, if used properly. Still, we're going to choreograph this in detail to make sure that there are no slips, no problems. Ready?"

And we did the same two minutes of fighting over and over and over. We started out slowly, walking through each move and working it, slowly adding a thrust here, a parry there, as Mr. Lombardi told us. At first I was a little worried that Jordan Paul might take advantage of this situation to try to take a little extra slash at me, to get back for me being in the lead. But it looked like it took all his powers of concentration to remember all the moves and make it seem remotely real and spontaneous.

It was very tiring. My legs and shoulders ached by the time Mr. Lombardi called an end to rehearsal.

I pulled on a hooded sweatshirt, and put my jacket on over it. As I expected, the cold air outside chilled the sweat on my face and chest, making it seem even colder.

Lydia was waiting for me at the path leading into the woods. She was sitting with her back against a tree, writing in that journal. She got up as soon as she saw me.

"What happened to your eye?" she asked.

I touched it. It stung where she hit me in the library. I wasn't sure if she was kidding or if she really didn't know that it was swollen because of her. I shrugged, leaving it open.

"You want to come over to my house?" she asked.

"You know, I really have to finish up that paper about point of view in *Gatsby*."

"I want to be with you," she said. "Come to my house."

"Mmm. I don't know." I didn't want to go there for a

few reasons. One was that I was still a little freaked out
by what happened in the library. It was definitely exciting, and I could still feel that kiss. But there were also the
things she said and the way she seemed so desperate that
made me a little nervous. And the hitting part didn't help
much, either. The other reason I didn't want to go to her
house was that criminal brother of hers who totally
creeped me out.

"Why don't you want to be with me?" Lydia asked.

"No, I do. It's not that. To be honest, your brother
makes me kind of nervous."

"Why?"

"Why? Well, just the way he's kind of threatening.
And all that house arrest stuff. I mean, what's up with
that?"

"Oh, come on. I was just kidding about that. He hasn't
been to jail. Yet." She laughed and pushed me. "Kidding
again. No. Really, there's nothing wrong with him."

"Really?"

"Really. I mean, nothing that his Thorazine and shock
treatments can't control."

I must have squinted at her, because suddenly I felt a
sting where she'd hit me. I guess I winced a little bit and
touched my eyebrow.

She leaned over and kissed my eye, softly and gently.
"Come on over to my place," she said. She switched over
to her Southern accent. "Come on, baby. I'll make it worth
your while."

She touched me with her hand, and I knew what she was promising. How could I say no?

❧ ❧

As usual, the TV was flickering in the living room. That woman, Lydia's sister or mother or whoever she really was, was in the kitchen. She was wearing a big bathrobe and men's slippers.

"Hi, Gertrude," Lydia said.

"Evening, Gertrude. Oh, you're that boy, Eric. No, Thurman."

"Ethan," I said.

"Oops, pretty close." She laughed. She was obviously drunk. "I think I'll call you Thurman, anyway." She laughed to herself and went back to the stove, where she turned up the heat under a pot with water. She shook a small cardboard box. "Look! I decided to cook. A nice home-cooked meal, for a change. Delectable mac and cheese."

It was too dark in this place, even though the kitchen light was on, and the TV screen flickered from the living room. Something about it was just so depressing that I didn't want to be there.

Lydia's mother-sister tore the top off the box, and the dry macaroni popped out and scattered all over the linoleum. "Uh-oh," she said. She got down on her hands and knees. I knelt down to help.

"Guess I don't know my own strength," she said.

I smiled and looked up from the floor. Her bathrobe had fallen completely open in the front. I was trying not to look, so I looked at her face to see if she knew how exposed she was. It seemed like she did know. She was staring me in the eyes, grinning. "Oopsy," she said.

I turned away, scooped up the rest. I wanted to get out of there, pronto.

"Oh, please, Gertrude. Don't embarrass yourself," Lydia said. "I'm going upstairs. Come on, Ethan."

I handed my handful of pasta to Lydia's mother-sister and got up off the floor.

"Thanks, Thurman. You're a doll."

I went to the stairs to follow Lydia, and I heard her brother call, "He's a *doll*. Hello, Dolly. We're so glad to have you back where you belong."

When we got upstairs, Lydia threw her backpack on the floor of her room. All of her books spilled out.

"That was a really pleasant display," she said. "I hope she didn't make you permanently impotent."

"I don't think so."

'That's good to hear," she said, and she grinned at me. It reminded me too much of the same smile her mother-sister had given me just a few minutes before. Lydia came over to me and put her arms around my neck. She started kissing me, slowly and carefully. I got this weird idea that she was playing the part of some seductress she'd seen in a movie. It didn't seem real.

She started to pull me over to the bed.

And that's when I realized to my surprise that I wasn't up for what Lydia seemed to be offering. I thought I would have jumped at this chance. And I still felt the charge she'd given me in the library. But I wasn't turned on at all. Something was definitely wrong, and I didn't know if I could go through with it.

"Um. You know what?" I said. "The rehearsal was really physical, and I'm totally thirsty. Any chance you could get me something to drink?"

She looked at me for a second. "Sure. I can do that." She went out and closed the door.

How was I going to get out of this without hurting her?

I heard Lydia's voice arguing about something with her mother-sister, but I couldn't make out the words. Just intense tones and hissing.

I paced her room. I rubbed my face in frustration and winced when my hand went over the eye she hit. I knew I couldn't handle her.

Peeping out of her backpack was that green journal. I listened for a second to hear if she was coming back up the hall. The argument seemed to be in full swing, not ending in the next few seconds.

No second thoughts. I grabbed that green book.

I flipped forward and stopped when I saw my name.

I spent some more time with Ethan. He has no idea what a great person he is. He's smart and he's sensitive. He's kind. He's even deep. He just doesn't know it. He isn't like any of the other boys.

Wow. Deep? Sensitive? On the next page:

> I love him more than I knew I could.
> Ethan is the one. I can tell he loves me.
> He hasn't said it yet, but I know. I know.

On the next page:

> I think of Ethan all the time. He's so
> good. I wonder if I'm good enough for him.
> I worry that he's too good for me. That
> he'll leave me. It makes me scared. I worry
> that I'm going to slip back into my old
> problems. But if he'll stay with me, he'll keep
> me afloat. Ethan will save me. He is the only
> one. He will save me.

Then, on the next page:

> I feel it in my blood, with every beat of
> my heart, this is my destiny. He came into
> my life to save me. I could carve his name
> into my flesh a thousand times. And I would
> do anything for him. I love him so much. I
> would die for him. I would kill for him.
> I would do anything to keep us together.

What? What the hell was that? I flipped the page.

Ethan Ethan Ethan Ethan Ethan Ethan Ethan
Ethan Ethan Ethan Ethan Ethan Ethan Ethan Ethan
Ethan Ethan Ethan Ethan Ethan Ethan Ethan Ethan
Ethan Ethan Ethan Ethan Ethan Ethan Ethan
Ethan Ethan Ethan Ethan Ethan Ethan Ethan Ethan
Ethan Ethan Ethan Ethan Ethan Ethan Ethan
Ethan Ethan Ethan Ethan Ethan Ethan Ethan Ethan
Ethan Ethan Ethan Ethan Ethan Ethan Ethan
Ethan Ethan Ethan Ethan Ethan Ethan Ethan Ethan
Ethan Ethan Ethan Ethan Ethan Ethan Ethan
Ethan Ethan Ethan Ethan Ethan Ethan Ethan Ethan
Ethan Ethan Ethan Ethan Ethan Ethan Ethan
Ethan Ethan Ethan Ethan Ethan Ethan Ethan Ethan
Ethan Ethan Ethan Ethan Ethan Ethan Ethan
Ethan Ethan Ethan Ethan Ethan Ethan Ethan Ethan
Ethan Ethan Ethan Ethan Ethan Ethan Ethan
Ethan Ethan Ethan Ethan Ethan Ethan Ethan Ethan
Ethan Ethan Ethan Ethan Ethan Ethan Ethan
Ethan Ethan Ethan Ethan Ethan Ethan Ethan Ethan
Ethan Ethan Ethan Ethan Ethan Ethan Ethan
Ethan Ethan Ethan Ethan Ethan Ethan Ethan Ethan
Ethan Ethan Ethan Ethan Ethan Ethan Ethan
Ethan Ethan Ethan Ethan Ethan Ethan Ethan Ethan
Ethan Ethan Ethan Ethan Ethan Ethan Ethan
Ethan Ethan Ethan Ethan Ethan Ethan Ethan Ethan
Ethan Ethan Ethan Ethan Ethan Ethan Ethan
Ethan Ethan Ethan Ethan Ethan Ethan Ethan Ethan
Ethan Ethan Ethan Ethan Ethan Ethan Ethan

And it went on like that for page after page.

I felt every part of my body get cold. My heart started going, and I felt that weird adrenaline rush. I had to get out.

I heard footsteps coming up the stairs. I shoved the book back in her backpack, making sure the corner peeked out, just like before. I stood up just as the door opened.

"Here's a Sprite. It's all we have."

"Thanks. But you know what? I have to go."

"What?"

"I really need to leave. I'm totally wiped out from the rehearsal. We worked on the swordfight stuff, and I really just want to get home and into bed."

"You're leaving?"

"I really have to."

"Did my mom freak you out? Because I just told her, and she'll leave you alone."

"No, it's not that. I just really need to go."

"Are you mad at me?"

"No. Of course not."

"I know I hit you before, and I'm sorry. I just got very excited."

"It's fine. Don't worry about it. Really. It has nothing to do with that. It's because I totally forgot that it's my sister's birthday today, and I forgot about it last year, and it turned into this whole thing. So I really can't miss it this year."

Lydia looked like she was going to cry, and I was pretty sure she wasn't acting. I couldn't come up with any decent excuses. And saying that I was just a little freaked out from reading her diary didn't seem like too good an idea.

"Why are you rushing out like that so suddenly? What's that about?"

"Listen. I'll see you tomorrow. I just really have to go," I said.

"You made a promise to me today. You said you won't leave me."

"I'm not. I'm just going now. Just for now."

"You promise."

"Absolutely."

She looked at me in a way that made me want to get out even more.

After she closed the front door, I forced myself to walk slowly up her street, just in case she was watching me. When I got to the corner, I turned back.

She was standing at the window, staring.

I waved and turned the corner.

As soon as I was out of sight, I took off. I ran all the way home.

COURAGE SINKING

I was out of breath when I got home. Everyone was just starting dinner. "What happened to your eye?" Mom asked.

"It's nothing. I got hit with a basketball in gym. I wasn't paying attention."

"Michael, take a look at that."

Dad took my chin and turned my head. "It's just a bruise. You can put some ice on it. Does it hurt?"

"It's fine."

"It makes you look tough," Amanda said with a smile.

"Great."

"Sit down and eat."

"I already did. I stopped on the way home. I just have a lot of homework." I went to the stairs.

"Everything okay?" Mom called.

"Yeah," I called from the stairs.

"Anything wrong?" Dad called.

"Just great." That was about five lies in less than one minute. It might have been a record for me.

I couldn't stop thinking about Lydia. She was turning

out to be much more than I could handle. Even before I read the diary, I was getting uncomfortable. But that stuff she wrote about her past problems and me keeping her afloat? Saving her? I was coming to the depressing conclusion that something was very wrong with her, that it wasn't just that she was dramatic or exotic, but that she was actually sick or something.

I was up all night. All the stuff was starting to get to me. I was struggling to keep my grades up. I was trying to keep all my lines for the play in my head, and all the repetition I was doing kept them swirling around in my mind, even when I didn't want them. I was feeling worse and worse about how I treated Jane. The idea of being disappointing to Amanda made me sick. And I was feeling guilty about the whole thing with Mr. Dugan. Even if he was a jerk, he probably didn't deserve what we had done to him.

So all this stuff kept me up all night, and I wasn't a pretty sight when I faced myself in the mirror in the morning after I took my shower. I opened the medicine cabinet and aligned the mirrors so I could get a look at my tattoo. It had still burned when the shower spray hit it, but not nearly as bad as before.

It was changing. There was kind of translucent layer over it, which the tattoo guy told me would happen. It was dead skin. It looked like the symbol was slipping under the surface of cloudy water. Courage sinking.

〜 〜

"Is that real?" asked a wrestler in the locker room that day right before gym.

"What?" I said, pretending I didn't know what he meant.

"The tat."

"Oh, that? Yeah, it's real." Acting totally cool.

"Pretty good. Nice work."

I left my shirt off for a while, pulled my sweatpants on, took my time tying my sneakers. I was pretty sure a few of them were looking at my ink, as those of us tattooed guys like to call it. So I just played it casual, cool as can be.

"Hey, Ethan. Let me see." It was Steven Chen, who was playing Ben Kwo in the play.

I turned my shoulder so he could get a better look.

"Wow. I didn't know you were so serious."

"What do you mean?"

"But it's spelled wrong," he said.

"It says 'courage.'"

"No, it doesn't."

"Or maybe 'bravery' is a better translation," I said.

"Yo, dude. It says 'Lydia.'"

"What? Very funny."

"I'm not playing."

"It says 'courage.'"

"It does not. I'm serious. It doesn't say anything close to 'courage.' It's a phonetic spelling. But it's more like 'Lee-da.'"

And again, I felt my body get cold as my heart sped up. And just like Luke Skywalker knew in his heart that Darth Vader's horrifying words were the awful truth, I knew that Steven Chen wasn't lying and that I had Lydia's name tattooed on my shoulder.

✺ ✺

"Are you fucking kidding me?" I shouted at Lydia in the hallway.

"It's nice, isn't it?"

"Are you out of your mind? How could you do that?"

"You're squeezing my arm pretty hard."

"Answer me! How could you do something like that?"

"It's easy. You just slip the guy an extra hundred bucks."

"This isn't funny."

"I agree. It's romantic."

"It's not romantic. It's . . . it's . . ."

"You need to let go of my arm. Thank you. Now what are you trying to say?"

I didn't know. I couldn't find the words to say what it was. Criminal? Psycho?

"Listen, Ethan. Think of it as a nice surprise. If you want, we can go back and you can get 'courage,' too."

"I don't want it now."

"But you need it."

I shook my head. I wanted to cry. I spoke really slowly. "Do you understand that I'm going to have your name tattooed on my body for the rest of my life?"

"Yes, I do." She looked at me with rain-cloud gray eyes, and she smiled. "I'll be a part of you forever."

✺ ✺

We were up to full-play rehearsals, and I felt like I was making a total disaster of it. I was so shaken up about the tattoo and everything that I went up on half my lines and had to get prompts from Megan Cordero, the stage manager. The AV guys were all over the place trying to figure out where they'd need to be to get the camera angles. I tripped about ten times on their stuff, which didn't help me concentrate.

I saw the looks that Mr. Lombardi and the others had, like they were wondering if I was going to cave and not be able to pull off the lead.

Even the swordfight between Jordan Paul and me was a mess. All my fault. "Okay," Mr. Lombardi said when we finished the final scene. "That wasn't exactly the energy I was looking for, but you guys have been working hard, so we'll call it a day. And tomorrow, I hope to see some lightning in here. I know you can bring it." We all clapped, but slowly, in a way that didn't exactly shake the auditorium walls. "Uh, Ethan? A word before you leave, please?"

Just about everyone left as I was taking my time putting my bag down on a front-row seat. Lydia was standing nearby, waiting for me. I gave Mr. Lombardi a look and flicked my eyes toward Lydia.

"If you could give us a few minutes, Lydia?" he said.

She nodded and walked up the aisle. After the back doors closed behind her, Mr. Lombardi turned to me.

"What's the matter?" he said.

"I don't know."

"Is it a case of nerves? Jitters?"

"Yeah."

He looked at me for a moment. "You don't lie well. Is something bothering you, outside of the play?"

"No. Why?"

"Because I'm watching you and I can see on your face that something is gnawing at you. Do you want to tell me?"

I looked at him. I liked him probably more than any other adult in the building, but I couldn't tell him. Since it was about Lydia, and he had to work with her, I didn't want to bring all of that stuff to him, into the show, and onto the stage. He was too connected. I wanted to leave him out of it.

"No. It's okay."

"That's not too convincing. But if you won't talk to me, maybe you can talk to the counselor or someone. Nothing wrong with getting some advice or guidance."

"Maybe I will." Not.

He clapped me on the shoulder. "And as far as the play goes, you know I have total confidence in you." I understood then why he had never made it on Broadway or in Hollywood. He was a rotten actor. I could tell he didn't have much confidence in me at all.

We shook hands, and he gave me an awkward kind of half hug. He went to check some notes with Megan Cordero, who had been standing by the wings, giving us some privacy.

I thought of Lydia on the other side of the doors at the back of the auditorium, waiting for me. I took off out the side exit.

༄ ༄

When I walked in, I heard Mom say, "Oh, perfect timing. Here he is." She held the phone out to me.

"Who is it?"

"Lydia."

"Tell her it wasn't me who came in."

"Oh, that's credible. I don't recognize my own son walking into my house."

"I don't want to talk to her."

"Why?"

"She's just weird."

"What does she want?"

"It's complicated. I'm not talking to her, though."

"Don't be rude." She held the phone to me. I took it and walked upstairs.

"I waited for you at the back of the auditorium."

"Oh. Well, I went out the side door."

"Why?"

"It's quicker."

"You're not avoiding me, are you?"

"No."

"Are you still mad about the whole tattoo thing?"

"Yes."

"Don't make a big thing about it."

Don't make a big thing about you tricking me into getting your name branded on my flesh? "Listen, I have a lot of stuff to do."

"Come over."

"I can't."

"Come over to my house."

"I'm not coming over."

"I want you to."

"I'm not."

"This is all about the tattoo? You're being a baby about it."

"I have to go now."

"I don't like the sound of your voice."

"There's no sound in my voice. It's been a long day and I'm tired and I still have a lot to do tonight."

"Okay. But I'm not letting you go until you say you're not mad."

"I need to go."

"Just tell me you're not mad at me, and I'll let you go."

"Fine. I'm not mad."

"Really?"

Not really. "Yes, really."

"Okay. Now tell me you love me."

"I can't do that."

"Why?"

"Because I can't."

"You can't or you don't?"

"Lydia."

"Is it you don't love me or is someone standing right there?"

"The second one." Coward.

"Okay. Fair enough."

"Do you love me? Just say yes."

Fine. "Yes." Let me hang up.

"I love you, too."

"'Bye."

Finally. I pulled my books onto the kitchen table. Mom took that as a signal that I wanted to work. She had a plate of leftovers from dinner that she pulled out of the microwave and put out next to me.

I was ten minutes into math homework when the phone rang. I made the mistake of picking it up.

"I've been sitting here, thinking and thinking," Lydia said. "And I really don't know if you meant it."

"Meant what?"

"That you love me."

I didn't say anything. I was getting mad again.

"So do you? Mean it?"

"I always mean what I say." I thought of the line that actors are professional liars.

"Really?"

"Really."

"Okay. So what are you doing?"

"I'm trying to get some homework done."

"You need to concentrate more in rehearsal."

"If I don't concentrate more on my homework, like right now, I won't even *be* in rehearsal anymore."

"Your parents wouldn't pull you out now."

"Oh yes they would."

"You know what? Let me talk to them. I bet I can convince them to get off your back."

"No. Just, no. Forget I said anything."

"I could help. I've helped before."

"Please just forget it."

"Okay, okay. Touchy, touchy, touchy. Just say it again before we hang up."

She's killing me. "I love you."

"That's what I like to hear." She hung up without another word.

I rubbed my eyes. I realized that I had a terrible headache.

And then the phone rang. "Don't answer it," I yelled to anyone within earshot.

But I heard it stop in midring. After a second, I heard Amanda call, "Ethan!"

"Come to the stairs," I called. She came to the top of the stairs, holding her hand over the mouthpiece of the phone. I looked up at her and made a cutting motion with my finger across my throat.

"It's Lydia."

I waved my hands like no-no-no.

"Hi, Lydia?" she said into the phone. "He just got into bed. . . . Yeah . . . Maybe he suddenly got tired. . . . Yes, it's true. . . . Okay, good night." She hung up. "She's kind of weird, you know?"

"Tell me about it."

"What's her problem."

"I don't even know. Listen, if she calls again, just don't answer it. Tell Mom and Dad not to answer the phone, that there were some prank calls."

"I told her you went to bed. You really think she'll call again?"

"I'd bet on it."

And I would have won the bet. She called a total of six more times that night, none of which we answered, but I knew it was her from the caller ID.

"Why does this person keep calling you?" Dad asked.

"She's just like that."

"Really. Sounds to me like she might just have a thing for you, huh?"

"You could say."

"What about Jane?"

"It's a long story. But I don't want to be with this girl."

"Okay, heartbreaker. But remember. Hell hath no fury, right?"

"Tell me about it." You don't know the half of it.

She probably would have called more, but we finally turned the phone off.

         ≈ ≈

I didn't walk by the pond on the way to school. I knew she would be there, waiting for me. I got a ride with Amanda and her friend Elaine.

I kept an eye out for Lydia, just wanting to get to class without bumping into her. I moved with the hordes in the hallway and suddenly felt a tight grip on my arm. It was her. She pulled me into the empty dance studio. The lights were off, and it was mostly dark, but I could see shadow images of us going on into infinity in the mirrors.

"I feel awful," she said.

"Why?"

"About last night. I'll admit, at first I was mad when you wouldn't take my calls. I know you were awake. But then I thought about it, and I realized that maybe I've been a little unfair."

"Unfair how?"

"Like the whole tattoo thing. I can understand why you're mad."

"Really?"

"Yes. And I'm going to make it up to you."

"How?"

"I'm going to get your name tattooed on my body."

Oh, man. "No. I don't want you to do that."

"I need to. To make this complete."

"You really don't. I don't want you to get a tattoo with my name."

"It's what I want."

"You know what? A tattoo isn't as meaningful as

people say. You know? It's just ink. That's all it is."

"Okay. Maybe you're right. So I could cut your name into me. That way your name wouldn't be ink, it would be a scar, it would be my own flesh."

I couldn't believe this was actually happening. It felt like I was acting in a horror story or something, but it had turned real. Altered reality, like, am I actually here in this situation? Is this really happening to me? Is this really my life?

"This is so beautiful. It's almost too beautiful for words," she whispered.

"What?"

"It's sublime," she said.

"What?"

"Sublime. It means pure and amazing. Awe-inspiring beauty. But in chemistry, it means to convert a solid substance by heat into a vapor. Isn't that weird?"

That's weird? Okay. "What did you think is beautiful and sublime?"

"Look at all of us." She pointed at all of our reflections. "We're alone and at the same time, surrounded by ourselves. Watching each other, watching us."

Her eyes were closed, her lips parted. "What if we made love, right here."

"What?"

She took me by the shoulders and backed me up against the mirror. It shook. She was actually pretty strong, and I worried that the mirror might shatter.

"Easy. This mirror could break," I said.

"And what if it did? What if we made passionate love on the floor, right on the shards of broken glass and silver."

"I think we'd get cut," I said.

"Yes."

"It'd probably hurt."

"Yes. But love hurts."

I was in way, way over my head. "Lydia. We have to end this."

"Yes."

"No. I don't mean it like that. I mean us. We can't go on like this. It's over."

"I know, I know. We'll have to part, and then our hearts will be broken. Forbidden love. Moving toward blood and violence, death and suicide and love all entangled like roses and vines."

There was a sheen of sweat on her brow. She bit her swollen lip, and her body seemed to shudder.

Okay, that's really it. Get me out of here.

"I'm going now," I said.

"Yes."

"Are you going to be okay?"

Her eyes were closed. Two big fat tears rolled slowly down her cheeks. And she was smiling. "Yes," she whispered.

As I closed the door behind me, I wanted to feel some sense of relief. But I didn't.

I knew that saying it's over didn't make it so. Not by a long damned shot.

⚘

FRAY

"I can see why you feel uneasy," Mr. Matone said. He had most of the same stuff on his walls that the other guidance counselors had: posters about making good choices. One said, ONLY *YOU* CAN CHANGE YOUR ATTITUDE! and another said, STAND UP FOR WHAT YOU BELIEVE IN . . . EVEN IF YOU'RE STANDING ALONE! Mr. Matone wore black jeans, a dark gray shirt, and a tie with pictures of Snoopy as Joe Cool, wearing black shades. His desk was covered with college applications and recommendations. Leaning against the wall were two electric guitars. There were rumors that he had been a pothead when he went to this same high school years ago, and now he played in some kind of band at clubs in the city.

Even with his tie and his feet up on his desk drawer, I didn't feel relaxed or comfortable. I was there because I didn't know who else to tell. I didn't tell him everything. The main thing I said was that I was involved with some-one, that we'd done some stuff I wasn't too crazy about, and that I felt pretty sure she was basically unbalanced. And I didn't know how to get out of this mess without causing a disaster. He listened and listened, and then when I stopped talking, he just watched me and made the comment about understanding why I felt uneasy.

"Well, what am I supposed to do?" I said.

"I don't know. What are your choices?"

"I don't have any."

"Really? Well that sucks."

"I can keep going out with her, or whatever it is we're doing."

"You like that idea?"

"Not at all."

"So what, then?"

"Well, I sort of tried to break up with her, but I don't think she understood. Or maybe she just didn't get it."

"Then maybe you need to tell her in a stronger way. So it's totally clear how you feel."

"That makes me worried. I think she might either turn on me, or, like, hurt herself somehow."

"You know, it would help if you could tell me her name."

"I can't. She'd flip out if she knew I told you any of this stuff."

"So what do you mean by her getting you to 'do stuff' that you're not comfortable with?"

"I'd rather not say."

"Was it sexual?"

"Not really."

"Criminal?"

"Not really."

"But you don't want to tell me."

"Not really."

He nodded a few times. He gently pushed his desk drawer closed with his foot and sat forward in his chair. "Okay, here's the deal. If you don't wanna tell me, don't tell me. But I can't do much to help you like this."

"I understand what you're saying. It's no offense to you, but I just can't tell you about some of this stuff yet."

"Up to you. But listen. If you think someone's in danger, you need to do the right thing. Be smart, okay?"

"Okay. Let me think about it."

"Fair enough," he said.

I left feeling worse and weaker than when I'd gone in.

∽ ≈

I was about to go into the library during lunch when Scott and Nora stopped me.

"You need to talk to Jane," Scott said.

"I already went through this with Tim."

"No, this is something else," Nora said. "Something's wrong."

"So why doesn't she talk to her new boyfriend," I said.

"We think it's about him. Something happened."

That got my attention. Suddenly, I went into alarm mode. "What do you mean, something happened? What's wrong?"

"We don't know," Nora said.

"Did he hurt her or something?"

"We don't know," Scott said. "She won't tell any of us."

"I'm probably the last person in the world she would want to talk to."

"I think you're wrong," Nora said.

≈ ≈

"You're about the last person I want to talk to," Jane said when I cornered her outside the cafeteria. My nerves were frayed, and I was in high-alarm mode.

"What happened?" I asked again.

"I just said, I'm not talking to you."

She tried to walk around me, but I got in her way. "Jane, what happened? Did he do something to you?"

"Why would I tell you anything? This is all your fault anyway."

"Fine. But just tell me."

"Why should I?"

"Because I want to help, and I won't leave you alone until you let me."

She glared at me and shook her head. "You're impossible. Whatever." She went across the lobby to the auditorium and tried the door. It was open, and I followed her in. It might not have been the most appropriate place for us to be together, considering, but at least it was private.

"What did he do to you?"

She shook her head again, and I could hear her working to keep her breathing under control.

"Did he hurt you?"

"Kind of."

"He hurt you? Like physically? Did he hit you?"

"Of course not."

"Did he . . . he didn't, like, force you to do anything."

Jane looked at me, confused.

"Like, he didn't . . ." The word caught in my throat. "He didn't, you know, rape you or anything, did he?"

"No."

"Jane, I can't keep guessing. Tell me."

She took a few more breaths, which came out ragged. "I'm making too much of a big deal about it. It doesn't matter."

"Just tell me."

"It was going okay with him. Or I thought it was. Then last night, we were, you know. Fooling around."

"You were?" Of course it wasn't fair of me, but I just felt totally jealous and disappointed.

"Yes, I was," she said, maybe with some "too bad for you" tone in there. Then I saw something else come over her face as she remembered it, I guess. "But then he kind of wanted to go all the way."

I swallowed. I was starting to feel sick.

"I could if I wanted to," she said. "You don't have any rights anymore."

"I know. I know that."

"So, he wanted to, but I didn't. And he got all pissed off and said all this crap about how the only reason he went out with me, the only reason he even looked at me at all, was so he could get back at you for taking his part in the play."

"But he gave it up."

"He still hates you for getting his part. And he totally used me and said all this awful stuff. How could I not see it? I'm such an idiot."

"Jane, the guy is a total player. Love 'em and leave 'em, that's what he does. You had to know that."

"You know what? You're not helping."

"I'm sorry. I just don't what to say. Except you deserve a lot better than him."

Jane nodded and pursed her lips.

"You weren't in love with him or anything, were you?"

"I guess not."

Good. "I could punch him," I said.

"He's bigger than you."

"So?"

"So he'd probably beat you up."

"So?"

She laughed.

"I deserve it."

"It's not you I want to get hurt."

"You know, he made a big mistake, letting you go. The biggest." Looking for trouble, I didn't stop. "I should know."

She looked at me. I was ready to take a good hit. Instead, she just kind of gave me a sad smile.

✺ ✺

I got a C on the English paper I wrote about point of view in *The Great Gatsby*. Ms. Wagner's comments were: "Much of this makes little sense. Did you proofread it? This is so disappointing. I know you can do much better!"

She was right. It was basically gibberish. I knew what I meant, for most of it, anyway. But it was like I had left out every other thought, so nobody else could possibly follow it. I'd worked on the paper late at night and hadn't bothered to read it over. I just hit print and was glad to be done with it. She was being nice by giving me a C.

I was slipping.

✺ ✺

The next thrilling event of the day was rehearsal, which meant quality time with Lydia. So I was getting a queasy feeling knowing that I was bound to have some kind of weird scene with my own personal psychopath.

"You didn't answer the phone last night," she said.

"Yeah, well. You have to stop calling me fifty times like that."

"It was thirty-seven times. And I wouldn't have to keep calling if you would just answer the first time. You know, I saw you with your ex-wife before."

"Yeah? So?"

"So I don't like it."

"You think I need your permission to talk to her?"

"Why are you getting so hostile?"

"Why are *you*?"

"I'm just saying. It's disrespectful."

Disrespectful? Was she kidding? "Disrespectful how?"

"To me."

"I thought I told you that I think we need to take a break."

"Well, I don't. So we're still together."

"I really don't think so."

"Think again. And I want to know why you went to the guidance counselor."

What the hell was this? "Have you been following me all day?"

"I'm keeping an eye on you."

"Why?"

"To make sure you behave yourself."

"Um. I think there's a word for what you're doing."

"Being in love. That's three words."

"No. Stalking. That's one word."

"It's the wrong word. Stalking is when you don't have a relationship with the person, but you imagine you do."

"Uh-huh."

"Very funny. And anyway, stalkers are usually seen as dangerous. Do I really seem dangerous to you?"

You want the truth or a lie? And the way she smiled, trying to look cute and innocent, only made her look more capable of acts of viciousness and violence.

"I can't keep doing this. I don't think it's good for either of us," I said.

"You don't know what's good for you. That's why you need me."

"I know that this is not good for me."

"Let's go, people," Mr. Lombardi shouted. "We have a show to put on very soon."

We were having a full dress and technical rehearsal, with all the lighting and film crews working. At the beginning, I was having a hard time getting with it. I was distracted by the film guys who were digitally taping during the on-set parts of the play, when our characters were acting on film. I was also getting thrown by seeing our scenes being shown in real-time on the monitors and screens that were built into the set. I'm sure it looked cool from the house, but onstage, I had to get used to it, and I kept losing my place in the play.

I heard Mr. Lombardi sigh a few times. He was getting nervous. But I wanted this; I wanted to play this part and do a good job. I just had to get totally into it, more than I'd ever been.

During the swordfight, I looked at Jordan and thought about how he treated Jane. When I made a thrust with my sword, he parried it, and the contact felt more solid than when we rehearsed in slow motion. I didn't want to overdo it and lose control. I knew that feeling the emotion was the way to my character. Mike Beath was angry and scared about his enemy trying to take what was his. I slashed at Jordan. He slashed back. He thrust, and I parried. He attacked and attacked, backing me up.

How much longer could I defend myself? I blocked every attack, but I couldn't do it forever. I was getting backed against a wall.

The sword flashed and whistled through the air. I couldn't block the attack forever. My heel was touching the wall behind me, and pretty soon I'd be slashed up.

No more backing up. Now was the time for action.

I drew my dagger and burst forward.

TURNAROUND

After rehearsal, I went to Jane's house. We talked in her father's study. I always liked that room in her house. Her father worked for a children's book publisher, and the room was filled with books. It smelled like leather and cologne.

Jane looked across the room at a framed poster of a picture from *Where the Wild Things Are* while I told her pretty much everything. I didn't go into too much detail about some of it. She got enough of an idea about what happened without having to get grossed out with the creepy details. She nodded a bunch of times, maybe even cringed a tiny bit once or twice.

"So were you, like, in love with her?"

"I don't know. I mean, no. I think it was more like this weird crush or something."

"Hey. I told you she was weird."

"You did. I should have listened to you."

"I always know," she said in a singsongy voice that wasn't quite as cheerful as it used to be.

"Pretty much."

"Why didn't you tell me that you cheated? On the tests, I mean."

"I guess I wasn't exactly proud of it. I didn't want to blow your image of me." She nodded to herself. "Did I? Blow it?"

"Well, it's different, definitely."

I looked at her. Even though all the stuff I told her made me look pretty bad, and there was a decent chance that she might decide in the end that I was a total zero, it was kind of a relief to tell her. It was like smashing a building with one of those huge wrecking balls, cleaning out the crumbly parts, and seeing what was still solid.

She didn't make any promise. But at least I knew there was a chance we might work things out.

❧ ❧

It was dark out when I left Jane's house and walked up the hill toward my street.

"Hey."

I almost jumped out of my skin. It was Lydia. She was just lurking there.

"What are you doing here?" I asked.

"Just taking a walk."

"That's pretty interesting. And you just happened to walk in Jane's neighborhood."

"Funny coincidence. Just lucky that way, I suppose." She had the Southern accent full-on. She stepped out of the shadow and under the streetlight. She looked bad, washed-out, and her hair didn't look right. Her eyes were puffy, and there was a little tiny stripe of blood on her chapped bottom lip where it was cracked. "I need to talk to you," she said.

"This isn't getting us anywhere."

"I just want to know what I did wrong?"

"Lydia, I don't know. I just don't think we're good together."

"But I'm the best thing for you. I know I am."

"You don't really know me. I think you have this made-up version of me, a fictional me, a mythical me."

"You know something? I think I may be the only person here who knows the actual you."

"Really. Well, whatever. It's nothing against you personally. I'll be honest, I was kind of falling for you."

She smiled at me, and I knew I'd just made a wrong turn. All I wanted to do was just end this quietly and peacefully. I just wasn't sure that I knew how. "You're really interesting, and you're smart and talented. You're a very . . . you're great, but I just don't think you're the person who's right for me."

"I could be that person, then. I could become that person. If you just give me the chance, I'll be whatever person you want me to be."

I felt really sad for her. She didn't even see how this was humiliating for her. She had this awful, miserable look in her eyes. I felt totally sorry for her, and I had to remind myself that she wasn't always like this, that she could be conniving and vicious, too.

She must have been reading the way I was struggling, because suddenly she looked more hopeful and took a step toward me.

"So you'll give me another chance?" she said. Her breath made a visible fog in the cold air.

"No. I really think we should just end it."

"We're not going to just end it. You may not understand this, but when things get a little tough in a relationship, you need to work on it. You can't just give up when there's so much there."

"But there isn't. There isn't so much. I'm not saying it's all your fault, but I feel totally stressed. It feels like being on a runaway train. It's too intense."

"You hate me."

"I don't hate you. I just don't want to go out, or whatever it was we were doing, anymore. I'm sorry, but I don't."

"And you get to make that decision."

"Well, I guess if one person doesn't want to, the other person can't force it."

"And I want to know what you told that guidance counselor."

"Just stuff."

"Like what? I want to know what you said about me."

"I said that I was worried that you would take this kind of hard. That you were kind of an emotional person."

"Oh, really? Is that right?"

"You don't think you're emotional?"

"Is that a crime?"

"No, but I was just worried about you."

"How touching. If you were really worried, you wouldn't be trying so hard to hurt me."

"See, I'm really not. Can we go to Mr. Matone together and maybe talk about this with him?"

"Oh, sure. After you made me out to be some lunatic."

"I didn't even tell him your name."

"Right."

"I didn't."

"I don't trust you. You *want* to hurt me."

"No I don't. I just want all this to be over. I want to make things right with Mr. Dugan, clear all that up. And just, you know. Move on."

"Oh, like I've never heard that before. Well, not this time. Not this time. Not without a fight."

"I'm not looking for a fight, Lydia. I just want both of us to be happy."

"How beautiful. You make me want to puke."

She actually bared her teeth at me. She looked like she might attack me. Instead, she turned and hurried away in the direction of her house.

I watched until she was out of sight.

∽ ∾

Lydia didn't show up for any morning classes. In the middle of social studies, Ms. Rosen's phone buzzed. She picked it up, listened, then said, "That's fine," and wrote out a pass. "Ethan, Mr. Matone asked to see you."

I went to the guidance office, wondering what the

deal was. I thought we had left it that I would let him know if I wanted to talk some more to him. I knocked on the door, and he called for me to come in.

He was sitting at the small round table, not at his desk. Sitting across from him was Lydia.

"What's going on?" I said.

"Have a seat, Ethan."

I did. There was something here I didn't like. His Batman tie didn't relax me. Nothing relaxed me.

"Lydia came to me with some concerns."

"Okay," I said. I wasn't picturing her going to him with a plan to make things easier.

"Would you like to tell Ethan what you told me?"

"You can," she said in a tiny little voice. Where was that coming from?

"Well," Mr. Matone said. He took a long breath. "It seems that Lydia has a very different perspective from you."

"In what way?"

"Lydia is saying that you've been pursuing her, even though she's made it clear that she isn't interested."

"What?"

"She says you've been following her, calling her, flirting with her. She tried to be nice, but now she's getting very uncomfortable."

"That's a total lie!"

"Well, that's what she says."

"She's lying! This is what I meant when I told you about her. She's the one I was talking about that time."

"Well, she's basically saying the opposite of what you told me. And she says you're scaring her now, and she doesn't know what to do."

"It's total nonsense. I'm pursuing her? She called my house like twenty-five times in one night."

"I don't even know your number," she said.

"I'm telling you, I don't want anything to do with her. She's the one who won't let *me* go."

"Oh, really?" Lydia said. She turned to Mr. Matone. "Why don't you ask him what's on his shoulder?" Her voice was shaking. She obviously was going for an Oscar or a Tony.

"What's on your shoulder?" he asked me.

"Now, hold on one minute."

"He had my name tattooed on his shoulder in Chinese."

"You made me do that!"

"How could I make you do that? I kidnapped you and dragged you to a tattoo parlor and forced you to get my name tattooed on your . . . body? Why would I want you to do that when I don't want anything to do with you?"

"You are out of your mind!"

"Is this true, Ethan? Did you really get Lydia's name tattooed on your shoulder?"

"Yes, but I'm telling you, it was her idea. She tricked me."

He looked at me in a way that made me realize how unbelievable my words sounded.

Lydia took a shuddering breath. "I mean, he's the one with my name tattooed on him, not the other way around. What more proof do I need to give that I'm the one telling the truth?"

Mr. Matone didn't say anything.

"This is total bullshit!" My voice cracked in a completely embarrassing way, and I knew I sounded hysterical. Crazy. Not helping my case. I took some slow deep breaths to cool down, and I was aware that I probably looked like a crazy person trying hard to pretend to be calm. I couldn't win. "Mr. Matone, I swear to you, I *swear* that I'm not interested in her. I don't want anything to do with her. I wish I'd never met her. I wish she would just disappear from my life." I wish I would just shut up instead of making this worse.

"Ethan, West Baring High has rules against sexual harassment."

"Sexual harassment?"

"If Lydia told you that she was not interested in you and wasn't comfortable with your advances to her, then every time you said you loved her, that you wanted to go out with her, that you wanted to have sex with her—"

"I didn't say those things."

"You never said you loved me?"

"No."

"Don't lie."

"Well, I did, but that was when you made me say it."

"I *made* you say it?" She looked at Mr. Matone, and he

gave her a look back, like he understood everything she was talking about now.

"Okay, okay," I said. "You want proof that I'm telling the truth? How about this. Why don't you ask to see her journal."

"Which journal is that?"

"Her journal. The green one. She carries it around all the time."

"She showed you her journal?" Mr. Matone says.

"Well, no. But I had a look at it this one time."

Lydia narrowed her eyes at me. I was pretty sure she wouldn't physically attack me in front of the guidance counselor. I knew that what I was saying didn't exactly make me look like a model citizen, but at least it would prove my innocence.

"Why don't you show him?"

"Because it's private," she said, almost in a hiss.

"Right. It's private. She doesn't want to show it to you because it goes on and on about how she's in love with me. It proves that she's lying and I'm telling the truth."

"Do you really have this journal he's talking about?"

"It's totally private. I don't show it to anybody."

"Well, I appreciate that. But it would be helpful in this situation."

"You'll have to take my word for it that he's lying. My journal doesn't say what he says it does."

"Then why don't you just show it?" I said.

"Because. There's a principle involved. It's private. You had no right to look at it."

"I would like to see it, Lydia, since it seems that it might settle this whole thing," Mr. Matone said.

Lydia slumped in her chair, her lower jaw came forward, and she dug in her bag and pulled out the green journal. "Can I at least pick the page to show you?"

Mr. Matone took it. "I won't read all of it," he said. He opened it and flipped through, stopping every so often. He cleared his throat. "This is from last month. 'This guy in my class named Ethan seems very nice, smart. He's pretty cute, too.' Then, let's see, a week later, 'I'm excited that Ethan got a part in the play. He's a very good actor. We'll have fun.' Then, hmm. 'This Ethan guy keeps following me around. He's becoming a pest.' Let me see."

What was that? Before I could say anything, Mr. Matone started reading again. "Here, 'Ethan keeps trying to be around me. He says he loves me and it's really getting creepy. I wish he would just leave me alone.'"

"What?"

"A few pages later, 'I'm trying to be sympathetic, but this Ethan is starting to scare me. He's like some kind of stalker or something. And he showed me that he got a tattoo of my name on his shoulder. I wish he would leave me alone. I'm worried that he's kind of crazy and might hurt me or something.'" Mr. Matone closed the journal and gently handed it back to Lydia. I almost couldn't talk.

"That's not her journal."

"Whose is it?" Mr. Matone asked.

"I mean it's not the same stuff I read."

"Sure. I got rid of it and wrote a whole new journal just for this meeting."

"See?" I said to Mr. Matone. I immediately knew how crazy and ridiculous I sounded.

"We need to find a way to reconcile this now, before this goes any further," he said. "Lydia, what would make you feel more comfortable?"

"Well, I guess I can't ask that he be transferred to another school. So I guess, if he'll apologize—"

"Apologize!"

Mr. Matone shushed me and turned back to Lydia.

"If he'll apologize and promise not to talk to me or bother me in any way, I could live with that."

"I'd be totally happy never to talk to you again."

"That sounds like an agreement," Mr. Matone said. "How about the apology?"

"Are you kidding me?"

"We're trying to make peace here."

"Fine, fine, whatever. I'm so sorry that I ever had anything to do with you. It's the biggest regret of my life."

"That's not exactly what I meant by an apology," Lydia said.

"Well, that's what you're getting," I said, trying not to shout.

"Okay, let's leave it at that for now," Mr. Matone said. "You can go. Lydia, you go first."

"Thank you," she said, oh so sweetly. She walked out and closed the door behind her.

"You can unclench your fists, Ethan."

I did. I hadn't even noticed.

"She's a total liar, Mr. Matone."

"You have to keep away from her."

"Do you believe me?"

"I think you should go back to class."

"I'm telling the truth."

"See you later." He went to sit at his desk. The hell with him. I went to the door.

"Watch yourself," he said. I almost said something I would have regretted, but I didn't.

When I stepped into the hallway, Lydia was standing there.

"You picked the wrong person to mess with," she said.

"How could you do that?"

"Hey, hey," she said. She held up a finger in my face. "You're not supposed to talk to me, remember?" She waved the finger in front of my eyes, watch out, and then turned and walked away.

It was all I could do to keep from attacking her.

Which was probably all part of her plan.

❧ ❧

"Mr. Dugan, can I talk to you?" I said.

"What's the matter, an A isn't high enough? Maybe you want me to write you a character reference for early admission to college?"

"I just want to talk to you."

He got up and walked into the hallway. I followed.

"I told you, I won't put myself in the position of being extorted by you again."

"Look, I just want to apologize. I want to make all this right."

"Of course you do."

"No, really. I'm totally prepared to do whatever I need to. I'll take the F. I'll leave honors chem. I'll take the suspension. I just want to set things right."

"Your sense of honor brings a tear to my eye. You'll forgive me if I don't believe you."

"Mr. Dugan, I'm trying to do the right thing. Can we please go into your room and talk."

"Let me guess. You'll grab my hand, make me touch you, and your little girlfriend will spring into the room with a video crew. Thank you, no. I've learned my lesson with you."

"I really would like to talk to you."

"That's unfortunate. I won't fall for this twice. And frankly, I don't give a damn what you want."

He went into the lab, pulled the door shut, and locked it

behind him. I looked through the little glass window. He was sitting at his desk, staring back at me, looking like a caged animal.

I shook my head and went down the emptying hallway. Last bell. I was late.

～ ～

I went to Jane's locker after sixth period. She was standing there with Nora. Jane did not look happy.

"What's up?" I said.

"You tell me."

"What does that mean?"

"What does *this* mean?" She waved a piece of paper at me.

"What is it?" I asked.

"I found it in my locker."

I recognized Lydia's handwriting as soon as I unfolded the paper.

> Dear Jane,
> You seem like a nice person, so I'm writing this to you to try to be supportive of you. Sometimes I think girls should stick together when faced with degrading male behavior, so I felt I should let you know some things.
> After making love, Ethan did not speak kindly about you. He said you were

a prude and stuck-up. He said that he couldn't connect with you emotionally because you were cold and uncreative. He was frustrated that you weren't involved in drama like we are, and he said it was another way you didn't understand him. He also said he couldn't relate to you because you weren't close to him intellectually. Sorry, but he actually said you were "kind of dumb" (sorry! His words!). I know it must be hurtful to hear this, and it feels terrible telling you, but since I heard these things, I knew he wasn't who he pretended to be, i.e. a sweet, sensitive, nice guy who was pretty smart (did he tell you about his academic dishonesty???) and I had to break up with him. I also felt that it would be the right thing to do for me to warn you about him and what he said about you.

Please forgive me, but he isn't the guy he seems to be and I'm just trying to help you from getting hurt the same way I did.

Sincerely,
Lydia Krane

"Okay, listen to me. This is all lies. I never 'made love' with her, never. And I never said those things."

"Do you think I'm dumb?"

"No! Of course not. She's crazy, I told you that."

"Well, the thing is, I know that I'm not in honors with you, and I don't do the play. And you told me that some of the things she mentions are true." She didn't say any more about it because Nora was standing there, but I knew she meant the cheating stuff.

"The important stuff isn't true," I said.

"Maybe we have different ideas about what's important."

"Okay, Lydia, listen."

She gave me a look like I'd just given up her family to bounty hunters. I realized what I'd just said. What a dummy.

"Jane. *Jane.* I'm sorry. I've just spent so much time arguing with this girl that when I get into this kind of argument, I just think of her name. I'm sorry. Listen. Please just listen to me for a second. I did not say those things about you. I don't think those things about you. It's all not true. Do you believe me?"

"I don't even know what I believe anymore."

And she walked off, leaving me alone.

Lydia had crossed the line this time. I mean, way crossed it. I thought of one of the best lines in the history of drama, the one that made clear that battle lines had been drawn and chaos would reign until the speaker emerged as

the victor. It was the unstoppable, unbeatable Bugs Bunny
who said: "Of course you know, this means war."

≈ ≈

"What's wrong with you?" Amanda asked.

"Nothing. I'm just sitting here."

"I know. Why are you acting like a zombie?"

"What are you talking about?"

She pushed my legs up so she could sit on my bed. "I
knock and knock on your door, and you don't answer.
When I come in, you're in a trance. So I repeat: What is
wrong with you?"

"I don't know. I guess I got myself in a big mess."

"What, with that girl?"

"Mostly, yeah."

"What's her problem?"

"You mean other than her being a total psycho?
Besides that, she's perfect. The girl of my dreams."

"Sounds wonderful."

"And I got in some trouble with Mr. Dugan."

"For what?"

I didn't want to say it. Amanda swept her hair back,
waiting. If I told her, I was going to blow her image of me.
And I really didn't want her to be disgusted with me, to
think I was a creep. But the lie wasn't working so well for
me anymore, either. Nothing was working.

"Well, you might say that I kind of cheated on a test."

"I might say that?"

"Well, yeah. I mean, I did."

"Oh."

"And it's not the first time."

"Oh." She stared at my doorknob, silent.

"Well, say something."

"You don't need to cheat. You're smart."

"Not enough."

"In whose eyes?"

I shook my head. "I don't know. But I did it. And Mr. Dugan caught me. My fault. That's all on me. But then I got involved in sort of forcing him to let me off the hook. Now he won't even talk to me."

"How did you force him?"

"Well, that's where Lydia comes in. It's really all pretty seamy and low. And now I can't get this crazy girl to stop ruining my life."

"Wow." She looked at the window. I watched her think for a couple of seconds.

"You're disgusted with me, aren't you?" I asked.

"No. Just surprised, I guess."

"Go on and say 'I told you so.' I deserve it."

"Why would I say that?"

"Because you warned me not to do it. You told me to stay with Jane, and not to mess with this girl. You told me not to be 'that guy.' If I had listened to you, none of this would have happened. So you definitely get to say I told you so."

"Saying that now won't help much. What are you going to do?"

"I don't know. What do you think I should do?"

"I think you should do what you think you should do."

"Thanks. That helps."

"You know what? It's great that you want my opinion and that you trust me. I mean, really. But soon I won't be around as much. When I'm at Harvard, you're going to be more on your own."

I looked at her, and she got blurry as my eyes started to fill.

"I can still call you. I mean, you'll have a phone there. Or are you saying you don't want to talk to me after what I just said."

"You know that's not true. I'm saying that I won't always be around and you have to start figuring some of this stuff out, to know what *you* want to do, and how to make things right."

"So you're not going to tell me how to fix these things?"

"No. Because you already know."

I looked at her. My eyes cleared. She was right.

I knew.

PREEMPTIVE STRIKE

Mr. Dugan looked totally surprised, maybe stunned, when he came into the room. Who could blame him?

"Have a seat, Mr. Dugan," said the principal, Mrs. Hartigan. She was kind of heavy, had short steel gray hair, and was pretty strict and mean, earning her the nickname Hard-on Again. "I'll make the introductions. This is Mr. and Mrs. Lederer. You know Mr. Matone, the guidance counselor. And, of course, your student Ethan Lederer."

Everyone said hello, and Mr. Dugan sat down. Mrs. Hartigan sat forward and leaned her elbows on the conference table. "I know someone is covering your class and you need to get back, Mr. Dugan, so I'll bring you up to speed. We're meeting at the request of Ethan. He told us that he cheated on your honors chemistry objective test, that you caught him."

"Um, yes."

"And he also told us that he made some kind of threats to you, though he refused to say what they were, and that he convinced you not to turn him in. Is that correct?"

Mr. Dugan looked back and forth between Mrs. Hartigan and me, like he couldn't comprehend what he was hearing. "Well, yes, it is. But we reached an understanding."

"Mr. Dugan, we don't bargain with our students. We'll need to discuss that later."

"It's not his fault," I said. "He shouldn't have to pay for what I did. I'm taking full responsibility for everything. It was all me." I didn't want too many details coming out.

"Well, then," Mrs. Hartigan said. She placed her hands flat on the table. "Both parents have been cooperative, as has Ethan, which we appreciate. Ethan has waived his right to appear in front of Student Court. Ethan, do you have anything else to say?"

"Well, I want to apologize to Mr. Dugan. I want to apologize to my parents, who never raised me to be like this. And just to say that I accept full responsibility for what I did. It was my fault, and I'll take the punishment."

"Fine, then. First, you'll receive a failing grade in chemistry for the marking period."

"That's fair," I said. I heard Dad swallow next to me.

"Second, you'll be removed from honors chemistry and placed in regular chemistry."

"Okay." I saw Mom slump a little more in her chair.

"And you'll be suspended for two weeks."

"All fair," I said, as if they needed my approval.

"Do you have anything to add?" Mrs. Hartigan asked Mr. Dugan.

"No, I don't."

"Fine, then. Oh, we do have one other issue. It's school policy that a student on suspension may not participate in any extracurricular activities. Ethan has been cast as the lead in Mr. Lombardi's play. Unless there are objections, I'm going to let Ethan be in the play. Since the performances begin the day after tomorrow, there isn't enough time to replace him, and it would be unfair to cancel the play and punish all of the other students. Does anyone have a problem with this?"

Nobody said anything.

"Thank you," I said.

"Don't thank me," Mrs. Hartigan said. "Because I'm not doing it for you. I'm doing it for the other students."

I nodded.

"The suspension begins now. Thank you."

Mom and Dad shook hands with Mrs. Hartigan and spoke to her quietly. I went to the door.

"Ethan, can I talk to you for a second?" Mr. Matone said. He took my elbow and led me to the door.

"Just so you know, I wasn't lying to you about her," I said. "I could show you phone records proving that she's calling us; I could explain everything to you. If I were you, I would look out for her."

"Maybe you want to tell me some more about this."

"You know what, Mr. Matone? Thanks, but I've been up all night telling my parents about everything. I'm kind of wiped out."

"How did they take all this?"

"Better than I expected. They weren't happy, and my mom cried. My dad did, also, to tell you the truth. I've never seen him cry before. But I know now that this was the right thing to do."

"What was?"

"Coming clean."

"Is that what you did?" he asked.

"Yeah. Didn't you hear?"

"I heard. But I also got the sense that somebody else was involved."

"I don't know why you think that."

"Call it intuition. And I also have an idea who that might be."

"This is all on me."

"Ethan, if someone else is involved, she needs to accept responsibility. Why should you shoulder the whole load?"

"Because I can take the heat for this. I started it, I made mistakes, and I can handle whatever comes."

"Can you?"

"Yes."

"I still want to talk to you about all this, Ethan." His tie had a picture of Daffy Duck frowning in frustration like he did right after saying, "You're despicable." He was standing in front of me, looking serious and concerned. I thought about his cartoon ties, and his guitars, and it occurred to me that he had a whole different private personality, too. Maybe everyone did.

"Maybe sometime. Right now, it doesn't really matter. Everything is going to be fine."

And I almost completely believed that, too.

∿ ∿

It was kind of weird in the car. Nobody said anything. I guess Mom and Dad were trying to figure out how to feel about the new version of their kid. The kid who wasn't exactly the ace student he appeared to be, who cheated on tests, who blackmailed teachers. The kid who seemed to be a certain kind of person, but was actually just an actor playing a part. I didn't say anything because I was trying to figure out how to be the new version. I guess I was trying to figure out how to be this version *with them*.

Mom was driving, and she had both hands on the wheel. Dad turned the heat up, then cracked his window, put his window up, turned the heat down.

Mom pulled up to the patient drop-off at the hospital. Dad turned around in the seat, took a quick look at me, then turned forward again. "We'll have to sort some of this out later. It's all very . . ." He cleared his throat instead of finishing his thought out loud. He shook his head, just a tiny bit. "I'm unhappy about the dishonesty, but I suppose I respect the fact that you came forward and did the honorable thing in the end."

"Thanks," I said.

"I'll be home late. I have a meeting at the medical

school." He kissed Mom and got out of the car to go back to work.

Mom pulled out of the turnaround and headed toward our house.

"Do you want the radio on?" she asked.

"No," I said. "I mean, unless you want it. Do you?"

"Oh, no, I was wondering if you did."

"It doesn't matter. Whatever you want."

"I don't care."

I looked out the window. It was getting even more uncomfortable.

"Oh, you know, you don't have to ride in the back. I can pull over if you want to get in the front."

"You don't have to."

"It's not a problem."

"I can ride back here, I don't mind. I know you need to get back to work."

"It would just take a second," she said.

"Fine. If you want. If you want to stop, stop. It's fine." She nodded, but she kept driving.

"This is difficult," she said.

I saw her look at me in the rearview mirror. I nodded.

"I don't really know how to talk to you now."

"I know." I could have said that I was the same person as I always was, but that wasn't true to her. I could have told her that she could still look at me the same way, but that probably wasn't possible. "I don't know what to say either."

We didn't talk for the next few minutes. This was the worst part of what I had done. I had really disappointed them, like, in a deep, deep way. I couldn't think of any way to overshadow that.

"So all of this makes me wonder something," she said.

"What?"

"Do you want to be a doctor?"

"No." Did I just say no?

"You don't?"

"Not at all."

"Is it that you want to become an actor?"

"You mean, like, for a job?"

"I suppose," she said.

"I don't know. I doubt it. It's just something I like to do."

"Do you have any idea what it is you'd like to do for a career?"

"Not really. When you were my age, did you know what you wanted to do for a job?"

"Yes."

"You did?"

"I loved lab work and science from when I was very little. I liked the order of it all. It was all very logical and clean. I guess it was a good match with my temperament, or the way my mind works. I really always knew that I would work in a lab somewhere."

"Oh. See, I just don't know. For me, I mean."

"I always knew, and I was completely driven by it. I

guess it never occurred to me that we were different that way. You don't know yet. You'll find it. Maybe we need to give you a little more time and room."

I'd never heard her say anything like that. It made me feel relieved, maybe even grateful. It made me suddenly feel closer to her. Almost made me feel like telling her I loved her.

Mom pulled into the driveway and left the engine running. "I'm going back to work. We need to think of some way to make this time you'll be spending at home worthwhile, so it doesn't seem like a vacation."

I slapped my overloaded backpack. "That's what I have all this work for." I got out of the car.

She waved through the window.

"See you later, Mom," I said.

❧ ❧

I wandered around the house for a little while before settling down on the couch to finish up the Fitzgerald book. That and the final paper on it would keep me busy for a while. I had plenty of math to do, a social studies unit and paper, and, of course, chemistry. I had stopped in the new chem class and met Mrs. Williams before I left. Almost everyone in there was a year older than me. That was fine.

The phone rang. Dad, of course, to make sure I wasn't just goofing off.

"I'm not watching TV," I said when I picked up.

"That's good," said Jane. "What's going on? They're saying you got suspended?"

"Yeah, I'm suspended."

"You? Of all the kids in this school, *you* got suspended? What did you do?"

"It's a long story."

"Let me guess. Is Lydia Krane involved in this?"

"Kind of. But it's really my own fault. I don't want to get into it now. Can I call you later? Or maybe stop by or something?"

"Okay," she said, without any hesitation at all.

"I have rehearsal, then I'll swing by."

"You're suspended, and they're still letting you do the play?"

"Nobody can learn all my lines in just two days. Jordan Paul never learned the whole part. Mrs. Hartigan said that just because I did something wrong, she didn't want to punish everyone else who was doing the play."

"That's fair. Wait, Nora wants to talk to you."

Nora got on the phone, and I had to tell her the same thing I told Jane. "That sucks. Wait a second," she said. "Scott wants to talk to you." So then it was Scott, then Tim. I had to repeat the story to all of them. Jane got back on the phone. "We'll call you seventh period. And I'll talk to you later."

"Sounds good."

The phone rang again in ten minutes.

"That was fast," I said into the phone.

"What did you tell those people?" Lydia asked.

"What?"

"I know you had a big meeting with the principal and your parents."

"Why did you write that letter to Jane?"

"Because it was stuff I thought she should know."

"What, you felt she should know a bunch of lies? We never 'made love,' and I never said those things."

"Maybe you didn't say them out loud, but you thought all of them."

"You need help."

"Look who's talking. I want to know what you said to the principal and all those people."

I knew it wasn't her business, and I didn't have to tell her. But she would have kept after me until she found out. And besides, I didn't want to feel like I was afraid of her.

"I told them that I cheated on the chem objective test."

"Are you a complete idiot? Why did you tell them that?"

"Because it's true."

"But I got you out of trouble with that whole thing," she said.

"Not really. Everything just got worse."

"What did you say about me?"

"Nothing."

"Sure. My name didn't come up at all."

"Right."

"You are such a liar."

I hung up the phone.

Before I got back to the couch, it started ringing again. I was going to let the voice mail pick it up, but it would have been too much like I was afraid to talk to Lydia, afraid to deal with her. If it even was her on the phone. So I answered.

"Nobody betrays me," she said. Of course, it was her calling back. "You think you can get away with this? Is that what you think?"

I hung up the phone again. It started ringing again almost immediately. I decided there wasn't much point in answering it anymore. There were six more calls before I turned off the ringer. I didn't even listen to the voice mails. I just hit erase.

We had another dress/tech rehearsal, and it was all looking really good. The video stuff looked really cool. Everyone knew their lines and was doing a good job. Jordan Paul was actually doing okay. Lydia seemed to be having a hard time with some of it. Instead of focusing on her work, she seemed more involved in giving me dirty looks all through rehearsal, but I didn't care. I'd cleaned up my mess, and I was taking my punishment. So let her be mad; let her think whatever she wanted. So what? What could she do to me?

ACTION

Of course, I was up the whole night before the play. I was definitely nervous about how I was going to do, this being the first lead I ever had. I kept feeling like I was forgetting my lines. I knew that trying to recite them, run them in my mind, wasn't going to help at that late date.

But the more I forced myself to stop thinking and to just sleep, the more nervous and anxious I got. At three-twenty, I got out of bed and went downstairs.

I looked through the cabinets, but I couldn't find anything good to eat. I didn't exactly feel like cooking something complicated. I scored when I found a fresh pack of Mint Milanos hidden in the back of the pantry I was halfway through the second little paper cup of cookies when I heard, "You found my secret stash." It was Dad. He sat down. "Did you leave me any?"

I pushed it over to him. He reached in and his hand got stuck in the sleeve. He finally tilted it so the paper thingy slid out into his palm.

"Why are you awake?" I said.

"I'm up a lot at night. You didn't know that?"

"What, like insomnia?"

"I suppose so. You, your mother, your sister—all of you sleep like the dead. Not me, though." He rubbed his thumb and finger together and let the crumbs rain down into the little paper cup. "Why are you awake? Nervous about the play?"

"I guess. That, and all the other stuff."

He nodded to himself. "I'm hoping that things will be better from now on. No more of that sort of nonsense at school."

"Never again."

He picked up another cookie and looked at it like it held some secret, the answer to some question. "So tell me. I pushed you too hard. Set the bar too high. Is that it?"

"No. You never told me to do what I did. That was me."

"But do you believe I forced you to that point?" he asked.

"I don't think it's about that. I just kind of always acted like the person I thought you wanted me to be. I think I got caught in the act. I couldn't tell who I was."

"You think you know now?"

"I don't know. I mean, I know who I thought you expected me to be, and I know who I tried to be. But I don't think I'm sure who I want to be."

"Not easy. It's how I felt when I played piano."

"When you what? You don't play piano."

"Not anymore. But I used to. Grandma and Grampy made me do it. They thought I might be a prodigy. They believed I could play Carnegie Hall one day."

"I can't picture it."

"Oh, sure. That's nothing. I was in a rock band for a little while."

"Get out!"

"It's true. It was called the Rubber Crutches."

"You have got to be kidding."

"I didn't stay in it long. I joined the band hoping that I would like it, because I never really got any enjoyment out of playing. And when I didn't even like playing in the band, I realized that I just didn't like playing music. And I haven't played in years."

"I never knew that."

"Now you do," he said. "But my point is that I played and played before I realized I was playing for other people and not for me."

"That sucks."

"It sure does. And this whole incident with you in school has really affected me. It really made me think. It makes me think that maybe I've been pushing you to play for me. In school. I'm sorry for that."

"It's okay."

He pushed back in his chair and stood up. "If you're going to play, play for you." He patted my shoulder and went upstairs to leave me alone.

I didn't feel worried anymore. I felt relaxed and comfortable. I had this feeling that everything was going to work out okay in the end.

❦ ❦

I slept a lot of the day away. I got up at two-thirty and took a good, long shower. I put on a T-shirt and jeans. My costumes were waiting at school.

I felt good, psyched up. Maybe it was coming clean about all the bad things I had been doing; maybe it was that I was going to try being less of an actor in my life, more real. Everyone would know about what I had done, about who I was. But for the first time, I didn't care what they thought about me. It was worth it to feel honest.

It seemed like I should mark it somehow. I looked around my room, and I knew exactly what would be the right thing to symbolize the new me.

Cloudy Boy had faded, but he wasn't going to disappear completely without a little help. Celluloid doesn't rip, I discovered. Not easily, anyway. But scissors work just fine. I left the thin strips of the X-ray in my wastebasket. Good-bye to Cloudy Boy.

❦ ❦

I got to school at five sharp. It was a tradition with Mr. Lombardi that we have a cast dinner before the first show. He always said it was so he could make sure that we all ate before performing, but I think it was more of a sentimental thing with him.

So there was pizza, some salad, a big hero sandwich cut up, and two aluminum trays of pasta. I sat by the food table with Steven Chen and two of the DramaRamas. Lydia sat with Jordan Paul, of all people. She was talking to him quietly, and he kept looking at other people with what I guess passed for a wry, amused smile on his face. After a while, he got up and came over to me.

"I need to talk to you for a second," he said.

"Okay." I put my plate and cup down on the table and followed him into the wings, the same exact spot where he had threatened me a while ago, saying I was trying to steal his lightning.

"Look," he said. "I just think I should say that we're about to do the show and that's really the most important thing. I was pissed that you got to play the part, but that's the way the ball crumbles."

"Bounces," I said.

"Yeah. And all that stuff with Jane Landau was kind of a way to get back at you and all, but whatever. I just hope that there's no hard feelings." He put out his hand. I shook it.

"You're a real good actor," he said. "Better than I thought." He couldn't exactly look me in the eye.

"Thanks. You are, too," I said.

"Well, anyways. Have a good show."

"You, too."

I went back to the table to get my food, and Lydia was pouring herself a drink. She cut her eyes at me and went back to pouring.

"Let me guess," I said. "You told him to say that to me?"

"Say what?" she said in a totally snotty tone.

"To wish me luck, and to say I'm a good actor and all of that."

"Actually, I didn't tell him to say anything. Believe it or not, we have better things to talk about than you." She twisted the top back on the soda. She gave me a nasty look and went over to sit again with Jordan Paul.

Whatever. I got my stuff and went back to talking to Steven.

A couple of minutes later, Mr. Lombardi stood up. "Okay, folks. We're getting down to it. We don't have much time. Actors, you need to get in makeup and costume. Crew, please get yourselves set up and test your lights. Film guys, let's double-check the video equipment and all the feeds to the monitors. I'd like to meet everyone backstage ten minutes before curtain."

I got in my costume for Act I, which was chinos, a black tank, and a red shirt over it. There were a couple of girls who were in the vocational program for cosmetology who helped us with our makeup. I got that fluttery, excited feeling while they did it. There was all that good, nervous chatter between all the actors, that good feeling of sharing this experience.

Megan Cordero, the stage manager, came back and called in, "Okay, people. Mr. Lombardi wants everyone backstage."

There were nervous smiles all around, and we headed backstage.

"Okay, gang. This is it. We have a good house out there. That was a good idea to get the English teachers to offer extra credit to all students who come to the play. Thanks for that idea, Megan. Now. I just want to make this short and sweet. I'm very proud of all of you. The actors, the crew, everyone. You've worked hard, and it's especially meaningful to me, as this is the first play I've written that's been produced here at West Baring. I am honored to have you present my work. So break a leg, everyone, and most of all, have a good time."

We clapped quietly for him. He smiled and went out to take his seat in the audience. The stage crew took off to the lighting cage; the video crew went to fire up their equipment. The actors all said good luck to one another; some shook hands and hugged. Actors tend to be kind of emotional. Lydia came over to me and leaned in. It was awkward, but I put out my arms to hug her.

"Don't even," she said. "I just wanted to tell you something." She leaned close to my ear. "I lied to you. You're not a good actor. To tell you the truth, you pretty much suck. The only reason you got this part is because I had a thing for you. I went to Lombardi and convinced him that you would be more interesting in the lead because you're so much *not* a leading man. And I told him that I would drop out if he didn't switch you and Jordan. You can think about that while you're onstage. Break a leg. At least."

"Oh. You, too. Please."

She had to wait until right before I was walking onstage to say all that. It was what I suspected, but didn't want to believe. Well, whatever the reason was, I knew that I had grown into the part. Maybe part of that was because of Lydia, or because she gave me confidence. Whatever. I was playing the part, and I was going to kick ass on that stage. Take no prisoners, I thought, as the curtain went up.

I knew by the middle of the second act that I was acting my ass off. I was into that character, and I was in the moment, all the way. Everything was working just right. Jordan was better than he'd ever been. Even Lydia was doing great, totally into the work, connecting with me like she was supposed to, character to character, person to person. I felt so close to all the other actors. I felt like we were connected on such a pure level.

I was all charged up with the acting.

I felt the edges of my lack of sleep fighting it out with my adrenaline stage rush. Every muscle was ready for action, every brain cell alive. I'd never gotten a stage rush this powerful before. I was able to focus on every single thing going on around me, every little nuance, every expression, all at the same time.

After Act III, I had to change into the black shirt. I was hot as hell, with all the lights and all the bodies in the audience. I had some water, but tried not to go crazy with it, since I couldn't exactly stop in the middle of Act IV for a bathroom break.

It was all going by so fast. We were up to Act V before I knew it. I was trying to enjoy all of it while I was acting, to feel the audience, to feel the other actors' actions and emotions. I felt tuned in to all of it. Lydia was wrong: this was the stuff only the best actors could do. Being aware of everything and using all of it. That was the name of the game.

I was getting giddy from the excitement of it all, from knowing that I had found myself, found the person I really was, the actual me. It was being onstage. It all felt right.

We were getting set for the last two scenes of the play. It was so hot onstage, I was all sweaty and thirsty. There were bottles of water backstage, and I had a little before going back for my next entrance. I happened to be standing with Lydia in the wings while Steven Chen, playing studio security, tried to halt the filming of the final battle scene of the movie in our play. He was arguing with Jordan Paul, and they were doing a great job. Our video crew was onstage as the film crew, setting up the feed. Everyone was perfect.

"I really loved you," Lydia said in a very quiet voice.

"What?"

"I did. Why did you have to break my heart?"

"I didn't want to."

"But you did. You did. But that's what love is all about, isn't it? Pain? True love has to hurt. Eternally."

"I don't know."

"I do."

She punched me in the stomach. It knocked the wind out of me a little, but it didn't really hurt. She shook her head at me, I could barely see her in the dark, but her eyes sparkled, wet. She hit me again a few times in the stomach. I reached for her hands to stop her, and she turned away. I barely felt the punches. I just felt bad for her.

"Come on," one of the DramaRamas said to Lydia. "It's our cue." Two DramaRamas got on both sides of her, put their arms around her. She let herself go limp and they carried her on, her feet dragging on the stage. They laid her on a cot upstage and explained how Lei-Dee had died of an OD.

I shifted my weight from foot to foot as I waited for my cue to go on for my big soliloquy.

"Does Mike know?" Bridget stage-whispered.

"Mike knows," Simone answered.

I went on and looked down at Lydia. The tears just came to my eyes and flowed like they had lives of their own. I gently touched her chin, and then I moved downstage, away from her. The lights came down low, and I started talking. "All the booze and pills. I guess it was going to happen sooner or later. If not today, then tomorrow. Tomorrow, tomorrow. If not tomorrow, then the day after. Life just shoots by and falls, disintegrates like old film stock, our images fading like celluloid ghosts. Life's just a washed-up hack actor, a silent film star, shuffling across the screen, shuddering, and stuttering as the film runs out, disappearing with the flickering light."

It was almost completely dark in the house, except for a spotlight on my face. I suddenly felt as tired and empty as my character, my energy leaking like blood from a wound.

I felt someone from the stage crew slip the sword and dagger into my hands.

"Roll sound!"

"Speed!"

"And . . . ACTION!"

Another spotlight blasted on, and I shuddered. There was Jordan Paul, moving toward me with his sword and dagger drawn and pointed at my heart. On the screen behind him was a video image of me, looking crazed, disoriented, the sword and dagger pointed down at the floor. I raised them and moved slowly toward him.

Just as rehearsed, we circled before we made those first moves.

He exploded toward me, slashing across with his foil. I blocked it, ducked, and spun away. I attacked him, and he blocked me.

We circled, attacked, retreated.

He slashed at me, I missed the block, and the foil just missed my face.

I saw my image behind him. I saw both of us on another monitor. I saw his face in front of me, slashing that dagger. I fought like it was for real.

We came to the last flurry.

He slashed down at me with his sword, and I blocked it with mine, holding, holding, the swords quivering over our heads. Holding, holding. I was drenched in sweat.

He made the stab with the dagger. I felt the tip touch me for a split second before it slid back into the handle.

I hunched over his fist and slowly, slowly lowered to the floor. He pulled back and left me.

I couldn't even hear the last words of the play, I was so into my own dying. All the sound bled into a buzz.

I was lying flat, my head turned away, so I couldn't see the audience. But I could see my image, my face up there on the screens. The strobe was going and flashed on and off, on and off.

That's me there.

My lips moved so slightly, slowly. My image big, the words loud in my mind.

That's me.

Me.

PSYCH

When I was a kid, I was expert at playing dead. I loved the dying scenes and played them over and over. Whenever the kids played War or Manhunt, I always loved the part best where I got to die. I was good at it. I didn't overdo it, but man did I make it real.

"You die good," kids would say. "You die the best."

That may have been the start of my drama career. I also acted out scenes from TV shows in my room before bedtime. It was then that I started to find out which scenes I could play best. I was great at the dying scenes, but after watching *ER* so many times, I was also good at the patient-with-a-serious-condition scenes.

I had played the scene so many times. Rehearsing without even knowing it.

I found out that all my memory starts again about six days after the play. I was conscious before that, but I don't remember any of it.

The doctors weren't as cool or good-looking as the ones on TV. They just looked plain, or tired. There were a lot of them.

"Ethan, are you still with me? . . . Right. You can't talk. There's a tube in your throat. Just listen. You needed some surgery, but you're going to be all right now. It's okay, don't worry. You lost some blood, and we had to do a little repair work. You know what your spleen is? Just squeeze my finger if you do. All right, that's okay. It doesn't matter, because you don't have one anymore. That was where most of the bleeding was from. Ethan? E—"

❧ ❧

Another doctor, younger.

"Does it feel better to have that tube out of your throat?"

"Yeah," I said. Talking felt like pulling a barbed wire up through my throat.

"I'll bet. Do you remember what happened?"

"Play?"

"Yes. During the play. Do you remember who hurt you?"

"I didn't get hurt."

"Ethan, you were stabbed six times."

Stabbed? Did he say I was stabbed? Was I dreaming or something?

"Easy, now. Don't sit up. You were stabbed six times. Your spleen was ruptured; your left kidney was pierced; your pancreas got nicked. All in all, it could have been worse. You're going to be okay."

"I don't know what you're talking about." I could barely recognize my voice. "I don't remember anything like that."

"It may be hard. You had some narcotics in your system."

"Can't be. Don't do them."

"Do you know what MDMA is?"

I shook my head. It hurt in my throat.

"You've heard of Ecstasy. That's MDMA."

Again, I shook my head.

"If you hadn't taken Ecstasy, you probably wouldn't have made it all the way through the play without either being aware of the stabbing or passing out."

"I didn't take any Ecstasy."

"You were loaded up."

"No."

The doctor looked at me.

〜 〜

Jane came. "You'll do just about anything for attention, won't you?"

"Just about."

"Just have to have the spotlight, huh?"

She smiled and cried. Then she took my hand.

〜 〜

"Amanda was here before, but you were sleeping," Mom said. She and Dad had been taking turns. Pretty much every time I woke up, one of them was sitting next to my bed, or looking out the window.

There was a knock, and a tall woman in a suit came in. "Knock, knock. I'm Detective Eckhart." She shook hands with Mom. It looked like they'd already met. "How ya feeling, Ethan?"

I made a half-half gesture with my hand.

"He's still pretty groggy with all the medication," Mom said.

"You up for a little conversation?" the woman asked me.

"I guess." I'd never talked to a detective before. What was going on?

"Okay," she said. "If you feel tired or sick, you let me know, and we'll stop. Okay?"

I nodded.

"Good. So listen. We need to talk about how this happened. About who stabbed you." She had a very calm, gentle voice. Not what I imagined a detective would sound like.

"Jordan Paul?" I said.

"No, it wasn't him. We checked out the dagger, and it was a prop. We looked at the tapes the camera crew made during the play. It was lucky we had them. The tapes showed us that Jordan Whiting definitely didn't have any other weapon in his hand."

"He was the only one who I had a battle with."

She and Mom looked at each other, then the detective looked at me. "We understand that you had some kind of a relationship with Lydia Krane. Is that right?"

"Some kind, yeah."

"Did she seem to be acting unusual around the time of the play?"

I laughed and then cringed when I felt lightning shoot through my stomach.

"She acted unusual all the time," I said.

Mom started to say something, but she changed her mind and looked out the window. I had a feeling she was going to cry.

"Well, we know what happened," Detective Eckhart said. "At approximately six forty-five, Jordan Whiting asked to speak to you privately. Do you remember that?"

"Yeah. He wanted to say no hard feelings that I got the lead role."

"Lydia Krane was the one who convinced him to talk to you then, to mend fences before the show. And so while you were talking to him, she put MDMA in your drink. You had a pretty good load on."

Lydia drugged me. That was why I felt so hot and electric during the play. That was why I was so thirsty. And I'd thought it was from the lights.

"You okay, Ethan?"

I nodded. It gave me a sharp pain in my stomach again.

She checked a small notebook. "Between acts, at approximately nine-fifteen, Megan Cordero witnessed Lydia Krane attacking you. You don't remember that?"

"I remember. She punched me a few times."

"She stabbed you."

"I'm telling you, she just punched me. There was no knife."

"She had an ice pick in her fist. We recovered it, and it matches the size and shape of your wounds. She stabbed you."

"Wouldn't I feel it if someone stabbed me?"

"The doctors say it might have been a combination of the excitement of the play and the Ecstasy, and you didn't realize it."

"Wait. So this was on purpose. She was trying to really injure me."

"The way she stabbed you? Ethan, she was trying to do a lot more than just injure you."

It was hard to believe that this was real, that this had actually happened to me, that it was my life. I remembered her saying something to me about true love, how it had to hurt forever. I knew there was something wrong with her, but I never would have guessed she was some kind of homicidal lunatic. If this was really all true, then Lydia actually tried to murder me.

"Ethan, you with me here?"

"Yeah. Why?"

"You looked as if you were fading out. So, you didn't get up from the stage floor when the lights came up for the curtain call. That's when they figured out something was wrong. They turned you over and saw a puddle of blood underneath you. It was actually Jordan Whiting who first called for help."

"Are you sure about all this?"

"We're sure. We have corroboration on all of it."

"Did Lydia confess or something?"

"I can't discuss that with you at this time," she said. "But I can tell you that her dying scene was meant to be for real. She was also loaded up on drugs. Ecstasy, barbiturates, the works. She was having a serious overdose, right there onstage."

She wanted to die with me. Even though I was lying down, I felt dizzy. "Where is she now?"

"She's in a special unit here in the hospital. But don't worry. She can't get to you. She's being watched."

"Are you completely sure she can't get to Ethan?" Mom asked. She turned back to us. Her eyes were red.

"Completely sure. She's in a locked unit."

"What's that, like a psych ward or something?" I asked.

"Something like that, yes. Listen, we're going to have a lot more questions for you, but you look like maybe you've had enough for today."

Definitely. I'd definitely had enough. I fell asleep before she even left the room.

∽ ∾

At night, I watched the little container at the bottom of the IV bag as each drop stretched before it detached. Drip. Drip. Drip.

After the nurse came at midnight to check me out and give me a couple more shots, I peeled back one of the dressings on my stomach. I couldn't sit up, so I couldn't see it so well. From that angle, I could see three tiny slits with one black stitch in each one. Then there was a big, long cut running near the edge of my rib cage, out of my view. I couldn't count all the shiny stitches. It looked like something out of a Frankenstein movie.

What a mess.

Talk about a bad breakup.

🌊 🌊

Mr. Matone came to visit me. He brought a bunch of magazines for me.

"Were you there when it happened?" I asked him.

"No. I had a ticket for Saturday night. You still owe me a performance."

It still killed when I laughed.

"I have to tell you, Ethan, I feel partly responsible for all this."

"You're not. She was a good liar. And then when you tried to get me to tell you more about her, I wouldn't. Not your fault."

"Well, I am sorry. It's a little late, but I was able to get some of her past records. It turns out she has a pretty significant psychiatric history."

"What was wrong with her?" I asked.

"A lot. She had features of what's called borderline personality disorder. It can be very serious."

"What is it?"

"Borderlines usually have intense and unstable relationships. They can latch onto someone and have power-ful attachments. But a lot of the time, their view of the relationship, and of themselves, is very distorted. They have an extreme fear of being abandoned or betrayed. They're very emotionally intense, and it's all or nothing for them. It's either love or hate, black or white."

"That's her, all right."

"Lydia had some other things going on. Some major family issues. I spoke to her counselor in Michigan."

"She was from Pennsylvania."

"She said that? No, she was from Michigan before she came to West Baring. She also lived in Cleveland, Boston. Let's see, Bangor, somewhere in Oregon, near Denver, she was in Virginia for a while. They moved around a lot. Seems like she and her brother had all kinds of problems, and the mother had to keep moving them around."

"Always on the run," I said.

"Sounds like it. They managed to stay just one step ahead of serious trouble."

"Until now."

"Until now, right. I don't know too many more details of what the problems were. Nobody seems to know the whole story."

That was for sure. I never knew the story with her. I probably never would.

≈ ≈

Mr. Lombardi came to visit. He mostly just sat there, looking miserable. He said he should have known better than to adapt *Macbeth*. It was often called the "Scottish Play" by actors who were afraid to say the title, due to its notorious history. Apparently, since the Globe Theatre, *Macbeth* has a startling record of productions that had bizarre backstage tragedies. I had become part of stage tradition.

Tim, Nora, and Scott brought about a hundred balloons each time they came.

And Jane came every day.

I got home sixteen days after surgery. They said I was completely stable.

CURTAIN CALL

I spent a lot time on the couch when I came home. I couldn't concentrate long enough to catch up with schoolwork. I was pretty much astonished when Mom and Dad told me not to worry about it. If I took an incomplete for the marking period, we'd deal with it later.

So I flipped through the channels on TV or watched DVDs. Just about everything reminded me of what happened. Any program that had a hospital story filled me with this sick feeling. I was off most of the painkillers, but seeing characters in hospital beds or crashing through the ER doors made me feel woozy and drugged.

I was amazed at how many shows there are that deal with legal stuff. The lawyers on TV made me think of the lawyers we'd been dealing with since the incident. They were convinced that Jordan Paul had no knowledge of how he was being used by Lydia. Since Jordan Paul didn't ever have much knowledge of anything, this wasn't too hard for me to believe. Mr. Lombardi wasn't held accountable, since the dagger in the play was, in fact, a harmless prop dagger, and he was as careful as he could have been to make sure things were safe.

So it all fell to Lydia, like it should have. The prosecutor hit her with charges of attempted homicide, endangerment, and assault.

It was two weeks after coming home, and I was in the middle of watching *The Godfather* for about the tenth time, when Dad came home with the news.

"Her lawyer got her some kind of insanity deal," he said.

"Meaning what?" I said.

"Meaning there won't be any trial. She's going to a psychiatric hospital in south Jersey."

It was weird, but I wasn't surprised, and I wasn't angry that Lydia wouldn't end up in some kind of juvenile-detention place. It just didn't seem like where she belonged. As she would say, it didn't seem like her fate.

"When is she going?" I asked.

"It's done. She's gone."

Gone. "That's it? It's over? That's the end of it."

"I guess so."

And just like that, it was over.

〜 〜

I didn't sleep well that night. I don't know if they'd even be called dreams, but I kept having these images of a girl dressed in black, in a small white room. There was nothing else in the room, just her, all alone. There was steam or mist in the room, and I couldn't see her clearly. I figured she was supposed to be Lydia, but her face was unclear, a blur. I had this feeling of restlessness. I was tossing and turning. I tried to relax, but sleep just wouldn't come.

It was four-thirty when I gave up. There was no way I was going to get any sleep. I got out of bed. I realized I was going to break a rule. Doctor's orders were that I wasn't allowed to leave the house alone for another two weeks, but there was somewhere I wanted to go.

I couldn't get the sweatshirt over my head. When I raised my arms, I still got a sharp stabbing pain where the stitches were. I did better with my coat. I slipped out the back sliding door.

A light dusting of snow had covered everything. The street was all white, not a single set of tire marks, sparkling under the streetlights.

My incision hurt, but it felt good to breathe in the cool air. I got there in five minutes.

The fog was so thick at the pond that I couldn't even see the other side. I couldn't see the surface of the water, if it had iced over, or if there was a layer of snow. All I saw was the fog. It was like staring point-blank into a cloud.

It was totally silent, completely calm and peaceful.

This was the place where I first told Lydia private stuff. This was where we talked about family, and about me, and about her. This was were it began, where we started to become close. Closer than I even knew. This was where the trouble started.

She was gone. I thought about that idea Mr. Lombardi told us about. The idea where every person feels like he or she is in a starring role, that other people are supporting players. In the play of my life, Lydia entered, played her role, and then she just exited. Gone. Just like that, she was out of the picture, out of my story.

The way she disappeared so suddenly, without a trace, it was almost like she had never been in my life at all. I didn't even have a photo of her. The only actual evidence I had that she ever even existed was the scars on my body.

But that wasn't true. I had other evidence.

Inside and out, I was different.

Mom said I could get the tattoo lasered off. It's true that the word on my shoulder isn't really "courage." But it doesn't matter to me what the letters say. It means much more than any one word to me. I'm going to keep it.

It may be crazy to say, but I don't totally regret the stuff that happened in my time with Lydia. If I could go back, there are a bunch of things I'd probably do differently. I wish I'd never hurt Jane. I wish I'd understood how much Lydia really needed help. And I definitely could do without the whole getting stabbed part. But I can't hit rewind, and I can't undo any of it.

I stretched my arms out and felt the sharp pain. But it wasn't as bad as before. I felt good. I was stronger. Getting better.

The fog was lifting. It was thinner, and I could start to see through it to the other side. Looking through the woods, I could see the light of daybreak starting.

❀ACKNOWLEDGMENTS❀

Thanks to all my family and friends who have encouraged me and shown interest in my work over the years.

Thanks to Regina Hayes for having confidence in this book, even when it was in a totally different form. Thanks to Anne Rivers Gunton for good ideas and lots of cheering.

Great big thanks to the greatest editor around, Jill Davis. You insisted on total honesty in the writing, made me dig deeper, and relentlessly demanded my best. You've helped me become a better writer.

Most of all, thanks to my wife, Ellen. You always believed, you always bolstered me. When things got tough, you smiled and stood fast. You're a great wife, a great mother, and a great source of patience, humor, and love. You've helped me become a better person.